About the author

As a new writer, Henry Regnault doesn't just use words to describe what he sees: he creates fun and excitement with a fast-paced story that takes the reader to somewhere new and unexpected and exciting. Henry created *The Three-Headed Dagger* series for readers to ask what's going to happen in the next book? Henry Regnault lives in Las Vegas, Nevada.

THE THREE WITCHES
AND
THE THREE-HEADED DAGGER

HENRY REGNAULT

THE THREE WITCHES
AND
THE THREE-HEADED DAGGER

Vanguard Press

VANGUARD PAPERBACK

© Copyright 2022
Henry Regnault

A CIP catalogue record for this title is
available from the British Library.

ISBN 978 1 80016 378 2

*Vanguard Press is an imprint of
Pegasus Elliot MacKenzie Publishers Ltd.*
www.pegasuspublishers.com

First Published in 2022

**Vanguard Press
Sheraton House Castle Park
Cambridge England**

Printed & Bound in Great Britain

Chapter 1
Tom Jones

*Oh, man, my head. What time is it? Where am I? Shit —
there is a lump next to me moving underneath the
blankets. Feels warm…* Cadence pulled them back. *Shit,
the girl is too young.*

The girl had long flowing brown hair with olive
skin and astonishing curves. She was around twenty-
five. *Did we? God, I hope so. Why can't I remember last
night? Shit, I need to get to the store so I can open up.
Where are my clothes? Ha! Scattered — that's a good
sign.* He looked around the room. It was small and dark,
one king-size bed, two nightstands on each side of the
bed, two lamps, an alarm clock, and a TV remote. The
room smelled old and musty. He could hear the roaches
scurrying around in the corners of the motel. There was
a stream of light peeking through the window curtains
to show Cadence it was morning. He gathered up his
clothes. Closing the door behind him, he was careful not
to make a sound and wake the beautiful girl.

Cadence Mage was over two hundred years old, a
slim five-foot-eight, with slight muscle tone pushing
through the skin. He was a beautiful man who made
women melt when they looked at him, but his beautiful

face had a worn, tired look — fighting demons for centuries will do that to any man. Worn or not, young women still turned their heads. His eyes were green, but not a typical green; they were lighter around the outside, pulling darker to the pupil's center. If you looked hard, you could almost see movement in them, like clouds on a soft, breezy day. When he turned the age of twenty, he stopped aging and became the demon hunter that he was destined to be.

Cadence opened the car door and slumped in the driver's seat. He stared up at the second floor of the Motel 6 and smiled. He crooked his head to one side and for a split second he thought he saw a shadow demon crawl along the outside wall; it looked at him quickly, then slipped inside the window where he had left the beautiful girl. Cadence shook his head, then turned the key in the ignition and started the car. He put the car into reverse, backed up, put it in drive, and pulled on to Fremont Street, heading for the I-15 freeway.

When the other car hit, the sound was a sickening crunch. Dark — low echoes — pain, head, side window, faint — slight breathing — DARKNESS…

***

Jell-O! I love hospital Jell-O. Nothing tastes better; it makes me forget about my head. I like the watermelon flavor the best, Cadence was thinking to himself.

"Hey there, hot and sexy, how do you feel?" Tom said, walking into the hospital room. "You were out cold for a while."

"Shit, Tom, how long was I out for?"

"Around three days." Tom knew Cadence would be upset at this. He needed his rest. Cadence never slept. He was always fighting demons in the dreamworld through the night, protecting the humans.

"Three days! I've been out for three days? Why didn't you get me out of this place sooner? Goddammit, Tom, I hope that Jenny has been opening the store on time?" Cadence searched around for his clothes.

"Relax, buckaroo, Jenny has taken care of everything. Don't worry. She's a great kid; she can take care of the store by herself. She treats that store like it's her own. That's more than I can say for you, my dear friend." Tom chuckled at what he had said.

"Yeah, you're right. I can always count on little Jenny. The store will be hers one day. Do you think she would like that? What do you think, Tom?"

"I think she will be thrilled; so please, stop worrying about the store. Let's work on getting you healthy so we can walk you the hell out of here," Tom Jones said.

Yes, you heard it right: Tom Jones. Everyone gave him shit about it, but Cadence did it more than anyone else. Tom wouldn't tell him, but Cadence guessed his mom might have been a huge Tom Jones fan or it was just bad luck that Tom's mother simply named him Tom.

That amused him every time he thought about it. Tom was a little strange, but had been a great friend to Cadence. Tall and thin, with short, wavy, light brown hair, he wore his pants too tight; Cadence thought he was gay, but Tom swore he was not. Cadence didn't believe him.

Tom walked into the store a little over ten years ago looking for a job. He seemed quirky and funny in his weird way and willing to take on any position in the store for work. Since then, Tom had been a loyal friend to Cadence and kept his secret all these years. Cadence was careless one day when he fell off a ladder and hit the back of his head on the edge of his office desk. He broke his neck and severed it from his spine. Tom was there and saw him come back to life and stand up. He never freaked out about it; all he said was, "That was crazy awesome, man."

Cadence was sitting up in his hospital bed. He arched his back, put his arms out, and his eyes rolled back in his head. Silence surrounded him, like when he stood under the hot water in the shower to separate himself from the world. Like the day his brother died. It was the only way he could feel he was alone. Then he heard a whisper.

"*I found you.*" No quicker than the whisper disappeared, his eyes opened. To his surprise, there was a beautiful face right in front of him, a glowing woman. She had long, flowing, bright red hair, thin lips, a perfect nose, and the bluest eyes he had ever seen. Her smell was slight honeysuckle with a hint of strawberries.

Her name was Heather! *God, she is beautiful*, he thought. Shit.

Again, she whispered, *"I have found you; I have been to all the long, damp, and dark places you have been hiding, and now I have found you. Now I am coming for you."*

"What the hell? Watching me and now she's coming for me?" Cadence said. "Heather, why are you watching me?"

"Cade! Cade! What's wrong? You OK?" Tom asked, trying to shake Cadence back into reality. "Let me go find the doctor."

"No, I'm fine." Cadence pulled himself up in the bed and ran his hands through his unwashed hair. "Get me the hell out of here, please. It's time for me to leave. Can you do that for me?"

"OK, I'll be right back. Put your clothes on and I'll check you out of here."

Tom walked around the corner to search for a nurse, his pants a little too tight. Cadence chuckled and said to himself, *"Why is Heather coming for me? Man! What was that girl's name from the motel the other night?"*

***

The store, better known as The Store, was left for Christopher and Cadence by their mother. Cadence had occasionally moved The Store when people were getting too close to discovering who or what he was. They always thought their mother loved them, but he always knew better. She left when they were young boys and were vulnerable to the evil that surrounded them. They searched for her through the years, but she was not on her own when she left. Christopher never recovered from that day; so Cadence took charge of The Store instead.

Cadence stared at Jenny, sitting behind the register, cleaning and polishing items before putting them out on the shelf for sale. He smiled and walked over to her.

"Hey, Jenny, thanks for minding the store for me."

"Uncle Cade, are you OK?" Jenny asked with a worried expression on her face, running over to give her uncle a big hug. "Tom said the crash was bad. You look terrible. I mean — this wasn't about dad, was it? Tell me what happened. I wanted to visit, but who would mind the store? Besides, Tom gave me all the updates on your recovery."

Jenny was cute, thin with pale skin like a vampire and long black hair. Jenny's father, brother to Cadence, had recently passed away. Cadence could tell she worried about him. She had lost her father and her mother a year before that. She was dependable, and opened and closed the store for her uncle every day without missing a beat. Cadence saw something in her, the way she glowed, and moved. He wasn't sure, but sometimes he would catch the way her anger grew. It formed into a faint light she did not regard because of her beautiful innocence.

Cadence walked into the back room where his office was. He turned on the sound system and flipped through some songs. *Oh, here we go, one of my favorites:* Just Like Heaven *by The Cure*, Cadence said to himself. *Ugh! A new book shipment.* He grabbed the box cutter and opened the top of the box. *Shit! More love stories. Why?* He threw the box aside and leaned back in his chair. His office had months of unpacked boxes piled in the far corner. The items on his bookshelf were caked with dust collected through the years, but he loved it and yelled at anyone who tried to straighten it out or clean it. His head hurt; he felt like his eyes would pop out of his skull. So Cadence turned up the music and went out front.

Jenny yelled out, "Turn that down! What the hell is that noise?" she asked, rolling her eyes.

"Aw, come on, that's not noise!" Cadence danced around like a geek from back in 1987. "Come on, dance with me; your dad would have liked that."

"Why? He is dead, and he is not coming back."

"I know, but let's have some fun now. Your father lived a full, wonderful, and healthy fun life. He created you, loved his wife, your mother — hell, he was happy when he closed his eyes for the last time. Let's cherish that, not mourn it." Cadence grabbed her arms and flung her around with him like a geek.

After the song, he hugged and told her, "It will be all right. You will be all right." Jenny smiled, looked up at her uncle, and hell — called him a geek.

Right then, the door opened and a thin, frail, older woman walked into the store.

"Oh, hello," Cadence said, letting go of Jenny, still wearing a smile. "How may I help you?"

"Well, young man, I am looking for a copy of Oscar Wilde's *The Picture of Dorian Gray.*"

"Oh, there are many publications. Why settle for that when you can read the original Lippincott monthly magazine? From the year 1890, when they introduced the story." Cadence searched through some shelves, wiping dust off some books here and there.

"Ah, yes, here it is. It was a lovely story when it first came out; it's a favorite. I know you will enjoy it as much as I did. Here, on the house, and if you don't like it, you can always return it for something else."

The older woman stared at Cadence, stared at his eyes; she found him very handsome, yet unsettling. She thought she saw a flicker of white-blue lightning dance around his pupils.

"I'm impressed you read this book, young man. They say it's a lovely story," the woman said.

"Well, thank you — matter of fact, I've read every book in this store two or three times, cover to back." With that, the older woman, satisfied with her free purchase, thanked him and left the store.

"Now, how are we supposed to make any money if you keep giving things away like that?" Jenny asked, sarcastically rolling her eyes. If Jenny only knew how much the items in the store were really worth. Cadence looked over at her and smiled.

Chapter 2
The Hallway

The hallway was narrow and long, lit by two dim light bulbs. One flickered; the other kept a low yellowish glow, like the tips of a heavy smoker's fingers from allowing the cigarette to burn past the filter.

At the far end was a faded blue door, paint cracked and peeling, the number nine, and a peephole.

A beautiful red-haired woman with blue eyes walked toward the number nine, gliding like there was no care except hers and only her existence. She wore a long black coat; her boots tapped with faint light echoes on the peeled-back linoleum floor. Slow… slow… she stood in front of the door and knocked with an elegant rapping of her hand.

"Who's there?" A voice could be heard from the other side of the door. Again, there was another graceful knock.

"Dammit!" The voice was annoyed by someone knocking on his door this late at night. The door opened to a crack.

"What do you want?" came the voice from behind the slightly open door. Right then, like from a dream, beautiful thin lips puckered like a kiss but blew lightly.

Black-gray smoke started from her lips and swirled around her and outlined her sexy figure. The black-gray smoke passed through the opening of the door. As fast as the woman disappeared, she appeared in the room next to Tom.

"*Are you Tom, Cadence's friend?*" a voice asked from inside Tom's head. Her lips did not move. She only tilted her head.

"Yes," Tom said with a nervous voice. "Who… who are you? How the hell did you get in here?" At that moment, the beautiful woman kicked Tom square in the chest. Tom flew back against the door and fell to the ground.

"*Hello,*" the voice said again in his head. "*Nothing personal, but I need Cadence's undivided attention.*"

Tom was lying on the floor in pain with confusion on his face.

"What… what do you want?"

The beautiful woman's boot came down hard across his face, splattering blood left and right. Tom felt the cartilage in his nose flatten through the inside of his cheeks. The beautiful woman kept kicking and kicking, with crunch sounds that followed each downward kick. The only thing Tom could see was a blur of a steel cross on the bottom of the beautiful woman's boot coming down on his face, slicing and embedding the symbol in his flesh repeatedly. All the while, the voice in Tom's head kept laughing. After it seemed like the nightmare would never end, the mysterious woman stopped and bent down.

"*If you live from all this fun we're having,*" she said, "*tell Cadence I am coming for him.*" A heavy sigh. "*Well, I had fun — how about you? Was it fun?*" asked the voice inside Tom's head. All the while, she kept smiling. Tom looked up at her through all the blood pouring down his face. *She is beautiful*, he thought. Another beautiful woman appeared in the room.

"Enough, Heather!"

Tom looked over at the other woman. She had long, strawberry-blonde hair that floated with every movement she made; her skin was smooth and had a milky color. All Tom thought was, *Wow, two beautiful women in my apartment.* The pain shot back through his brain, bringing him back to reality. Heather was still kneeling over him while looking at the other woman standing there.

"*Well, there she is. Hello, my sweet little sister, where have you been hiding? We've been looking for you. When I finish with Cadence, we will come looking for you next.*"

Heather stood up and stepped over Tom. She glided gracefully down the dimly lit hall until she disappeared.

***

A worried expression was on Cadence's face as he sat by Tom's side at his apartment. The place was small and had bright pastel colors everywhere. The floor had a blonde wood color; there was not one speck of dust anywhere in the apartment, and there were various pictures of him, Jenny, and Cadence on the walls and countertops. Sunflowers were placed throughout the room, only further elaborating on Cadence's theory that Tom was gay. Tom's face was a mess — barely recognizable. Cadence's thoughts drifted back to when he was a kid. He remembered his mother yelling at him because he cried that his brother Christopher hit him.

"Cadence! Stop crying. You are getting too old for that!"

He pulled his arm angrily away from her grip. "Just leave me alone!" Cadence rebelled. Smack! His cheek was left burning like fire ants were biting him repeatedly. Why was he thinking of his mother? He did not understand. He loved her, missed her, and wanted his mother back. Emotions built up inside as white-blue lightning licked around his eyes; a tear escaped and streamed down his cheek. Tom whispered something.

"*I am coming for you.*"

"What?" Cadence asked, and leaned in a little closer.

"*I am coming for you.*" Tom fell unconscious again.

Cadence leaned back in the chair. *Heather — what does she want? Why does she keep messing with me?* Cadence put his hand on Tom's forehead, then on his chest, to make sure everything was fine; he then leaned back in the chair again and tried to make sense of what happened at the hospital and what Tom had just whispered.

***

Cadence slammed open the front door to the store and walked down the hall with long, quick strides, passing all the aisles shelved with old and new books, antiques, and everything from swords, daggers, guns, jewelry, and everything else he had collected through the centuries. He stormed into the back office and sat at his desk, head in hands. Cadence breathed slow and cumbersome, keeping himself from screaming. "OK, what is going on here?" he said out loud to himself. Jenny startled Cadence as she walked into the room.

"Hey, Uncle Cade, how is Tommy doing? So, a woman kicked the shit out of him, huh?"

Cadence looked up at Jenny, laughing at what she said. "Yeah, he will be all right. His face is a little messed up, though." Cadence thought for a moment. "Hey, come with me, Jen. I want to show you something."

"What is it? Show me what?"

"I think you're ready."

"OK, ready for what?" Jenny stood with her arms out, looking bewildered.

Cadence looked at Jenny, raised his eyebrows up and down a few times in quick motions, and then formed an evil smile on his lips. "Ready to learn about our family secret? Why, of *course* you are. Come on, follow me."

"Wait, let me lock the front door and add the 'Back in thirty minutes' sign." She ran to the front of the store, locked the door, and turned the sign. She then ran back to her uncle's office, where he was waiting. Cadence turned to look at her.

"All right, are you ready to hear about an adventure of witches, demons, immortality, and how your family fits in all of that?" Cadence smiled.

Chapter 3
The Story

Cadence led Jenny to the back of his office. He moved the cover from the left eye of the small shrunken head he had found in South Africa decades ago. He pushed the hidden button behind it. The secret wall opened up slowly, a slight scraping sound with dust falling and mixing with the air. A set of stairs attached to gears pushed out down toward the basement, until it finally came to a complete stop, the opening leading into the darkness.

"Where did this come from? How come I never knew this was here?" Jenny asked with an expression of bewilderment on her face as she poked her head into the dark. Cadence turned in her direction.

"Wow, really — a secret door. I guess it's doing its job," she said.

Shaking his head with a little snort, he walked past Jenny, disappearing into the dark. "Follow me inside, and please — touch nothing."

She walked inside as the darkness engulfed her. Once inside the room, Cadence walked over to a podium at the center of the room.

"Jenny, please, sit there. I'm going to tell you about our family history mixed with a dark story. Now listen carefully. This will be a fun story, so don't interrupt."

Jenny's eyebrows arched up. "OK, well, I'm all ears."

"Your dad and I, well… we were born in 1801. We are over two hundred years old, and we are immortal."

"All right, stop right there. Already this sounds ridiculous," Jenny said, sounding a little annoyed.

"I know it sounds like that. Please, just keep listening."

"Where did all this old stuff come from?" Jenny asked, looking around the room. Statues and ancient weapons surrounded them. There were gold coins, gold bars, and money from many countries piled up waist-high on the floor in one corner of the room. Dust and cobwebs were everywhere, and in the center of the room stood a podium, backlit with a soft white light. A single book lay open on the platform of the podium.

"Well, I wouldn't call it old stuff. These items are ancient and priceless."

"Doesn't that word mean they are old?" Jenny asked sarcastically.

"All right, all right, can you just listen to the story?"

"OK, well, go ahead. Tell the story already."

"Well, that's what I am trying to do. Here, take my hand; let me show you."

Jenny reached out and grabbed her uncle's hand; her head flew back as visions swirled around. Blood ran between them both, through their noses, eyes, and ears. At that moment, time slowed down. Her uncle's voice slid through Jenny's head, flowing with sweetened mellifluous honey.

"Our mother — well, your grandmother — was into some dark witchcraft shit. Your dad Christopher had discovered this. He was fifteen, and I was twelve years of age. He grabbed me out of my bed to go with him to follow our mother one night. She was creeping down the basement stairs, and when she got to the bottom, she was talking with someone — something. It was a deep, bellowing voice. We followed, and when we got to the bottom, a dim light illuminated around the corner. Then we heard the voice."

***

Year 1816

"Now it's time for you to come back to me, Isabella. It's been too long."

Christopher rushed into the room, but no one was there, only their mother. She turned and yelled at Christopher. "What the hell are you doing here?"

Christopher looked dumbfounded. "I-I don't… we thought we heard someone else here in the room with you."

"We? Is Cadence here with you?"

Cadence stepped out from the shadows, his head down with embarrassment.

"Sorry, mother, Christopher made me come with him," he whimpered, pointing a finger at his brother. A bluish flame slammed into view and illuminated the entire room.

"*Ah, the boys!*" said the blue-purple flame. "*ISABELLA! Are these the young boys you spoke of?*" The flame danced around as it spoke.

"Yes, these are my sons. They know nothing; they won't understand." The boys looked up, as the walls were moving in closer and closer. Bones fell straight down, then flesh; wet flesh, skulls, arms, legs, and rib cages fell, hitting and cutting them. Blood was dripping down their arms, shoulders, and faces. Then, at that moment, as fast as it started, it stopped!

Christopher yelled out, "Who are you, and what do you want with our mother?"

The blue-purple flame danced as it yelled back, "*Who are you to question me — BOY? It seems no one taught you any respect.*"

"Leave our mother alone!" Christopher yelled back, not backing down. The blue-purple flame reached out and grabbed Isabella by her throat and lifted her off the ground.

"*Would you prefer I snap her neck and bite off her head here in front of you, boy?*"

Tears streamed down Christopher's face.

"No!" Cadence yelled. "Please stop, put our mother down. Don't hurt her; we will leave. We are sorry; we didn't mean to follow her and upset you."

"Yes, the smart one… Isabella, you were right about this one. What would you do for me if I let her go, boy?"

Christopher suddenly ran at the blue-purple flame with a rage of anger. "Let our mother go!"

The blue-purple flame turned toward them. Christopher suddenly stopped. It seemed like he had smacked into a brick wall and flew backward, falling to the dust-filled ground. Blood streamed down from his nose. He looked at Cadence.

"Hmm, how about a trade, boy? What do you think, Isabella? Should we play a game?"

"Please — ack, ack — please leave my sons be and put me down; you are hurting me," Isabella said, choking from the large hand wrapped around her neck.

"Boys!" said the blue-purple flame. *"I want you to search for your mother — search hard. Through time you may find her, and if you succeed, rewarded you will be, and you may discover who I am. Until then, her soul will be with ME!"*

When he took her, their lives changed, forever. They never figured out who the blue-purple flame was, and for almost two centuries, the boys had searched for their mother, only to come up empty every time.

***

"I have a question," Jenny said.

"OK, hit me with it."

"If you and Dad are immortal like you say, then how did Dad die?"

"He didn't want it anymore; he was tired. He just… gave up. He watched everyone die around us, and we just kept living. When he met your mother, he fell in love. After she died, it crushed him. He couldn't and wouldn't let her die alone. It would have put him over the edge seeing his daughter die. It never ends. It's like a loop: older people out, young people in, that's how the loop works. So, he wanted out — out meaning he would never get to find our mother and be released from the damnation inflicted on us by the blue-purple flame. All he told me was that he had found a way out. I told him I didn't want to hear it because I had to stay and take care of you and Tom."

"So, you're not sure how Dad died?"

"No, I'm not. Now, Jenny, please listen carefully. There are three dark witches the blue-purple flame summoned. They held us both under a light spell. Now that your dad's gone, all the binding spells disappeared, and they will come for me and come hard, so we need to prepare for this. Your dad discovered who the three witches are before he died. We know who they are, and now I have to find them."

"So, you know who the witches are?"

"Yes, they are called the Locke sisters. I know the woman who attacked Tom is Heather. The first of the three, they say, will come for us one at a time, and the next one will be stronger than the last. Yes, I know who they are. The youngest sister and I were in love over a century ago; her name is Meadow. Jenny, I know this is hard to breathe in all at once, but if you don't believe me, here is a very rare dagger. Stick me — ah, here." Cadence pointed to the area of the heart.

"You're an idiot. I don't want to stab you," she said, shaking her head with her arms folded in front of her.

Without hesitation, Cadence plunged the dagger into his chest, penetrating the heart. A burst of blood shot out and sprayed the statue in front of him, and a little got on Jenny's face.

Jenny screamed. "What the fuck did you do? Uncle Cade!"

Jenny heard her uncle laughing as he slowly pulled the dagger back through his chest, bone, and muscle. The skin pulled out with a sound of raw meat slapping the concrete ground.

"So, what do you think, Jenny — convinced?"

"What the fuck! What the fuck did you just do?" Jenny was turning in circles with her hands on her head in disbelief.

"Come on, Jen; I'm not comfortable with you talking like that." Cadence looked at Jenny with some disappointment on his face. "I'm sure your dad wouldn't approve, all the same. So, what do you think? Cool — huh?"

"That was disgusting," Jenny said, her face scrunched up with the look of disgust that absorbed her face. "OK, now I have a *lot* of questions."

"I know you do, Jenny. I'll answer as many as I can."

"All right, here's one. Did you and Dad duel with swords and wear those funky long boots that go up to your knees?" Jenny chuckled.

"All right, stop it! I should have never trusted you with the family secret. Man, and here I thought you were ready."

"Oh, shut up!" Jenny said with a crooked smile from the corner of her mouth. "Does Tom know about this, and why are you telling me this now?"

"Yes, Tom knows. He discovered my secret years ago; I was careless. And as for why I am telling you now? I feel there is a strong presence coming along with the three witches. I mean to destroy them, and Jenny — I will need your help."

"My help? What can I do to help?" Jenny was trying to make sense of what her uncle was suggesting.

"Yeah, Jen, your help. Your bloodline flows from this family; you will have powers. What those powers will be, that's what we're waiting to discover."

"Wait, I have powers, and Dad knew about this?"

"Yes, they just haven't developed yet, and when they do, I need to teach you how to use them. So… what do you think of the family? I know it's a lot to soak in."

"Let's see, can you kill yourself again?" Jenny said as she worked out a snort.

"Jeez, Jen, only once a day."

Chapter 4
First Dagger

"Jenny, I'm going out for a drink or two. Please, can you lock up the store for me?"

"Yeah, sure, I do it anyway," Jenny yelled from the back room, shaking her head.

"Man, another hot night; that's what I get for living in a desert," Cadence said to himself. He was walking down the alley when he heard someone barking out orders.

"Everyone, please keep moving, stay to one side, and stay behind the yellow caution tape; there's nothing here to see. Everyone, go home." As he ambled past the crime scene, Cadence turned to his right. There she was. Her beautiful dark-brown hair was long and flowing as it whipped around gracefully in the heavy, dry, hot winds; a light rain followed. She was thin, her jeans skintight, complimenting her curves. Her eyes were a dark blue-green that enlightened the face of the dark-haired, beautiful woman. Oh, and she looked pissed off. Cadence stared at her uncomfortably.

Cadence broke his stare and glanced over at the body on the ground. The body was lying in a small parcel of desert behind the Four Queens Casino off

Carson Avenue. The parcel of land was being readied for construction. He noticed the dagger sticking out of the poor girl's chest. While the police were busy pushing back the crowd and not paying attention, he lifted the caution tape and walked toward the body; he knelt, looking at the dagger, remembering.

***

Year 1819

A small town, Peillon, France, perched on a cliff outside of the French Riviera: population 546. It had been three years since their mother disappeared. It was cold and wet that day, and food was scarce to come by. People were starving and sleeping on the streets.

"Well, hello, handsome."

Cadence looked up. He was fifteen years old, awkward and scrawny-looking. *She is beyond beautiful,* he thought, thin and curvy with long, flowing, wavy bright-red hair.

"Who are you?" he asked, while hiding from the officer as he ducked behind piles of trash stacked in the alleyway, his head down on his knees. With a slight laugh, she reached down and pulled a dagger from a body's chest lying on the ground. As it came out, it made a quick wet sound like a kiss from two sets of lips pulling apart with heavy saliva.

"Why, my name is Heather, little darling; my, you are yummy."

Cadence stared at the dagger she held in her hand. The handle and pommel were formed from a human bone, and the sharp blade was made of black steel with three etched lines that followed the edge up. The blood wiggled and flowed up the first etching toward the handle. At the top of the handle were three skulls facing away from each other. In the center of the three skulls was a dull gray stone placed flat to fill in the space between them. When the bloodstream reached the handle, the first of the three skulls attained the blood; the knife glowed.

Heather slowly looked over at the boy; she smiled. *Oh my, that smile is beautiful*, Cadence thought to himself.

"You are one of them, beautiful little boy — you are one of them, aren't you?" With that, gracefully, she walked away softly and beautifully. Cadence scrunched his face, trying to understand what she meant.

***

Present Day

"Crap!" Cadence shook his head back to reality. He stared down at the body on the ground. While kneeling, he grabbed the hilt of the dagger and—

"Hey! What the hell are you doing? Who are you, and how did you get behind this side of the taped-off area?"

Cadence shifted his eyes up without moving his head; he felt nervous. She seemed scary.

"Who… me?" Cadence pointed a finger to his chest.

"Yeah, you. How did you sneak past the officers? OK, I'll tell you who I am. I am Lieutenant Anne Black, but you call me Lieutenant."

"Are you sure?" Cadence said. "I *like* Anne."

"Just tell me who you are!"

"Ah, I'm nobody, just walking by, curious about the crowd," Cadence said, pointing. "I saw the dagger."

"Yeah," Anne said. "Not hard to miss — kind of sticking out of this girl's chest."

"Well, I've seen this dagger before, if you're interested. It's old."

"I'm aware of how old it is." There was a hint of anger in Anne's voice as she rested her hand on the Glock holstered on her right hip. He loved watching her mouth with every word coming out of it; it made him feel… light-headed.

"There are at least five hundred folds on the blade, and counting; that's thousands of years old," Anne said. Cadence stared at her; his head tilted with a smile. He loved that she knew this.

"You know your daggers." Cadence sounded elated.

"Yes, I do. You can't be here, and I hope you didn't touch that knife? You are contaminating this crime scene."

Right then, Cadence bent back. His body arched, almost folded in half. His eyes rolled back into his head.

"What the hell are you doing?" Anne yelled out.

"*I am coming for you. You will remember — soon.*"

Cadence bounced back with a heavy, loud gasp!

"What the hell just happened?" Cadence asked, panting deep and heavy.

"Really? That's what I want to know. Are you some kind of a freak?"

"No, I don't think so. I was going for a drink, that's all." He looked over to his right and saw a beautiful woman with bright red hair and a half smile on the corner of her mouth. She drifted in and out through the crowd, as if no one noticed her. Cadence looked away, and over at Anne. She was pointing at him and talking with another officer about something. Then he turned back, but the bright-red-haired girl had disappeared. He shook his head and walked away.

"Hey, you! Stop! I want your name and number, in case I need to speak with you for further questioning," Anne yelled out to Cadence.

"Mm, yeah, whatever. I'm going to The End of the Street — a bar right down the street from here. The rain is picking up, and I want to hurry and get there. Be smart; bring the dagger along with you. It is unique — very rare. I'm not privy to the complete story, but I can give you some insight into it. Then you can have my number. My name is Cadence Mage." He turned away and walked down the wet street toward the bar.

"Weirdo!" Anne turned around. "All right, everyone, this is a crime scene, not a block party, so move on; nothing more to see here."

Cadence stopped in front of the bar, looked up at the blinking neon lights, and thought about the dagger from all those years ago. How could that be the same dagger? How did it get here? Most importantly, why was it here? Was it just a coincidence? He reached out and pushed the door to the bar open and walked in.

Chapter 5
First Witch

"Hey, Chase, where is everybody?"

"Not sure, Cade, it seems like it's just you and me tonight," Chase the bartender said.

"Fine with me, that's the way I like it. Can you get me a glass of wine? I've had a rough day."

Chase was beautiful, blonde, and thin-faced, with worn lines around her eyes. She was twenty-eight years old; they would sit for hours talking. She'd had a tough life. Her stepdad made sure she wasn't a virgin past thirteen. Her mom couldn't accept that her husband was having more fun with her daughter than with her. Cadence wished he could come across her stepdad. He would show him he was a virgin in some areas he didn't think possible.

The End of the Street was a bar like it sounded. It was at the end of the street, where the scum and dregs drag themselves from sunup to sundown each day. The place had been there since the old Mob days when Bugsy Siegel ran the town. Inside, there was an L-shaped bar that took up most of the room except the back area where the pool table sat. The bar was old and worn from all the fights, blood, vomit, and liquor that had spilled over from the bar to the dirty, sticky floor, but Cadence loved it. Nobody knew him there, and no one went there. The bar was where he went to relax his thoughts. Chase walked over and put a glass of wine down in front of Cadence.

"So, Cade, when are you going to ask me out?"

"Hahaha, Chase, you know you are too good for me." Cadence lifted the glass to his lips, and right then, the dagger hit the countertop. It slid and stopped in front of him.

"So, what can you tell me about this knife, Cadence Mage?"

"You mean this dagger?"

"Fine, what can you tell me about this dagger." Anne was rolling her eyes. "You cried out the name Heather when you were bent over, and shit — who is she, what does she have to do with this?" Anne barked.

***

Year 1819

The beautiful red-haired woman walked down the streets of Peillon. The first of the three witches turned the corner into an alleyway. There were damp and dancing shadows with a heavy smell of liquor, vomit, and smoke rising all around. An enormous figure was standing in the shadows. Its skin was hard and scaly, with red-orange glowing scales and black eyes set back deep in its skull. Shadows were rising all around the creature standing there; there was no clear view of its face, only the outline of horns stabbed into the skull. The horns stood up at least two to three feet high, surrounded by a blue-purple glowing flame.

"So, what news do you have for me, witch?" it asked in a deep, slow growl — so deep you could barely understand what the creature was saying.

"I have it all under control," Heather said.

"You do not have it under control! Do not forget that when I found your father and you girls, he struggled teaching you the dark powers; I did that for you. So, don't you lie, bitch! Tell me what you know!" yelled the blue-purple flame in a low, antagonizing voice. Heather's eyes widened from the echoes bouncing off the alley walls.

"The boy just happened upon me. He was hiding from the Flics patrolling the area. He saw me retrieve the dagger," Heather said. "He is the younger of the two; he is the one you want. He didn't suspect a thing." Fear set in her eyes and a bead of sweat rolled down the side of her temple.

"Yes, the boy is the key to all this. When the time is right, get what I want and then kill him and his brother!" The blue-purple flame grew large and loud, then slowly disappeared.

****

The door to The End of the Street opened; a beautiful red-haired woman walked through it, like in the movies, slow motion, then she stopped. She and Cadence stared at one another, like Clint Eastwood and Lee Van Cleef in *The Good, the Bad and the Ugly.*

Anne was the first to speak in the uncomfortable situation. "OK, who the hell is *she*?"

With no emotion, Heather turned to Anne. "Well, honey, if you're that interested in me, and you are yummy, I will show you who I am!" Heather's hand shot out. Her fingers spread apart, shooting white-blue lightning from the tips toward Chase.

"No!" Cadence screamed, and jumped toward Chase to break the lightning beam coming from Heather's hands. It seemed like it took forever for Cadence to get there, but he missed the beam when he did. Heather grabbed Chase by the throat with the lightning beam. She lifted her off the ground and choked her with the lightning. Heather's head tilted to the side, and in one quick motion she snapped Chase's neck. Her body went limp as she exhaled her last breath. A clear bright tear fell from her beautiful cheek and splashed to the ground. The sound of the teardrop was louder than anything else in the room. Chase stared straight ahead with a blank stare, motionless.

"God, no! Chase!" Shaking with anger, a force of energy surged through Cadence's bones, then his muscles, and straight through his arms, surrounding his hands. "Goddammit, Heather!" Cadence held his arms straight out, his fingers spread. Blue veins were stretching around his eyes, showing rage! Lightning! A vast lightning glow shot out from his hands and hit Heather. She was lifted and smashed hard against the wall, and tile and plaster flew in all directions. Dark blood flowed from her mouth.

"Hahaha!" A gross, disgusting laugh came out of her, along with a wet gurgling sound, like loose saliva mixed with thick blood and bile.

"Do you think you can hurt me, Cadence?" Heather grossly slurred.

"Well, I think I just did, dumbass," Cadence barked back. There was a heavy wheeze, like air pulling in and something blocking the passage, with a quick sigh from Heather.

"No, you haven't. I don't understand why my sister has been in love with you for all these years. This information will disappoint her. We all tried to convince her for years you were not the one for her. How disappointed she will be. How upset with the lies, and the deceit, with all the evil that flows through your veins. Now I know — I know who you are, *Demon Hunter*."

Cadence stared at Heather in silence. How did she know? How did she figure out that he was the *Demon Hunter*?

Anne dropped to her knees, arms crossed in front of her eyes, to shield herself from the swirling blue lightning that was suddenly exploding from around Heather.

"Ah, shit!" Cadence grabbed Anne and pushed her to the ground to shelter her from the blue lightning cascading around them.

"So, that's Heather," Anne said, looking up at Cadence. "Can you please get the hell off me?"

He looked down at her. "Yep, that's her."

"Well — do you mind?" Anne asked.

"No, not at all."

Anne gave a heavy sigh, looking up at him. Her upper lip curled back in anger, and she calmly said, "Well, do you think you could get the HELL OFF ME?"

"Oh! Yeah, right," Cadence jumped up and extended his hand to help Anne, but she brushed his hand away and stood on her own. "Sorry!" Cadence looked back over at Chase. He ran over to her motionless body. He fell to his knees and pulled her close in his arms, tears welling in his eyes; he slid her hair behind her ear and kissed her forehead.

"Chase, no — no, I'm so sorry. I should have protected you."

"Yes, you should have, but you failed her, Cady," said a sickening voice. Anne was getting sick and tired of this bitch.

"Heather, why? Goddammit, why? You wanted me! Why kill her?"

"I did that just for fun. This place bores me."

Rage formed inside of Cadence, and this time, a lot of rage! His fists were glowing white, blue, orange, and then instantly went dark black!

"What do you sisters want from me?"

"I want my dagger back, and you dead!" Heather said, laughing.

"No, I don't think I will give it back; you left it for me to find. Why don't you tell me who the blue-purple flame is? I know you know who he is."

"You will find out. Don't worry your pretty little soul. You will meet him soon."

Heather flew swiftly toward Cadence with a bolt of dark smoke lightning wrapped around her. To avoid being hit, Cadence dropped to one side.

"Screw you, witch!" All the energy and colorful lightning built up all around him. The colors mixed with the anger in him, thinking about Chase. His hands shot out with all the power he had; it hit Heather with rage. She flew back and hit the wall where there was a spike with a ball on the tip, to hang the guests' coats. It went through her skin, backbone, heart, and out the front between her breasts with a loud thwack! Heather groaned from the pain.

"You — why did he choose you? What is so special about you?" Heather croaked.

"Tell me who the blue-purple flame is!" Cadence screamed at her.

"Go to hell!" A drool of spit mixed with blood broke away from her bottom lip and slapped on the ground. She breathed out with a sickly wheezing sound. After a few moments, she did not breathe again.

"How did you do that?" Anne asked.

Cadence went back over to Chase and sat with her. "Please call 9-1-1; she didn't deserve this. She was an innocent in this." Cadence pulled her close and moved her hair away from her face. He kissed her forehead, rocking her back and forth.

"I am sorry about your friend," Anne said.

"Why are you sorry? You didn't know my friend."

Anne flushed red and stepped back. She stared at the ground, feeling a little embarrassed and shameful.

"She was like a daughter to me." Cadence pulled Chase close again.

***

Thirty Minutes Later

"OK, you've got my attention," Anne said. "I really am sorry about your friend, but I am still trying to wrap my head around what happened here tonight."

Now the bar was swarming with the LVPD and forensics. Cadence was watching them put Chase into the ambulance as they latched the back doors and drove away. Anne stood next to him, her hand resting on his shoulder.

"Come with me," Cadence said. "I can explain all of this."

Anne turned toward Cadence. "Fine, lead the way." Her eyes went wide, as if looking for something. "Do you know where the dagger went?"

"No, I do not, but we need to get back to my store."

***

"Shit, I thought Jenny had this lock fixed." He hit his shoulder against the door with a slight force. There was a cracking sound of wood, and the door opened.

"You sure this is *your* store?" Anne said. "I don't want to arrest you for breaking and entering."

Cadence looked back with a half-smile and a snort.

"Yeah, it's my store. It's dark; here, take my hand."

"In your dreams, freak."

"What's wrong with you? Who pissed you off at an early age?" Cadence asked, while shaking his head. "Yep!" he said after a few moments.

"Yep, what?"

"Yep, here is the light switch."

"Where are we again?"

"I already told you, we are in my store."

"OK, what kind of store is it? It looks like a junk store, like straight out of *Sanford and Son* or some shit like that," Anne said, with her lips pinched tight and one eyebrow up.

"It's a store; you know, old antiques, books, swords, and knives, stuff like that."

"I didn't know you knew how to read?"

Cadence hit the second light switch.

"Well, Doctor Seuss helped me a little, but the *Hardy Boys* and *Nancy Drew* novels got me through my adolescence. I'm sorry I had to keep you in the dark for a little bit. I didn't want you to see where I hide my secret room." Anne rolled her eyes as she descended the stairs, following Cadence into the darkness.

"Oh my god, what is this place?" Anne searched around the room, eyes wide, mouth slightly open. She had an evil face grinning from ear to ear.

Throughout the room there were ancient artifacts, money, gold, and treasures in all the corners. At the center of the room, she had to step around the piles, careful not to step on or break the precious items. It was a little chilly and damp, with a musty smell and cobwebs everywhere.

"Well, this is where the party starts." Cadence turned back and smiled, noticing the excitement on Anne's face.

"Why is it so cold in here?" Anne asked, wrapping her arms around herself.

"My artifacts need to stay in a cool environment."

"Yes, right, I should've known: sixty-eight to seventy-two degrees."

"Great, where do you want to start?" Cadence asked.

Anne looked at him with her doe eyes. "I don't know. Is this going to hurt?"

***

"Do you have the dagger?" Anne asked with a mean glare and a heavy sigh.

"You know I don't. I don't know where it went." Cadence walked over to a row of books on shelf D — D for dagger — and turned to a particular page. "Here, look."

Anne came over and sat down in front of the book. Cadence stared down at her exposed neck, smooth skin. He stretched over to smell her dizzy, heavy, intoxicating fumes. He felt a little light-headed. Anne pulled back.

"What the hell are you doing?" Her face was slightly twisted with silent amusement.

"Oh, I'm sorry." Cadence shook his head. His lips formed a straight line, like he was thinking. "Ha!" Cadence yelped, as Anne jumped with surprise. "Here, look here, in the book." Cadence's excitement annoyed Anne even more.

"What am I looking at here?"

"See, the dagger. The book is calling it The Eyes for the Souls." The picture showed a single black blade with three etched lines leading to the handle. The pommel had three skulls, each facing out. Cadence glanced over at Anne.

"Why do you seem a little annoyed with this information I'm showing you?" Cadence asked.

"Why? Because you still haven't explained how you threw that woman — what's her name? Oh, yeah, Heather — you threw her across the room into a spike hanging on a wall without touching her."

"Well, I hope that impressed you?"

"Shut up! Just tell me how you did it."

Anne's cell phone rang and broke her stare and annoyance as she answered the phone. Cadence heard her talking to the other person, and then things slowed down.

"Do you think you can hide from me? I know who you are. You will know who I am soon!"

"Hey! Cade — you OK?" Anne stared at him. One eyebrow went up, and I mean high up — she looked hot! "I have to go back to the bar and deal with the dead girl stuck to the wall. I will deal with you later. We need to sit and go over this dagger situation. What's the name?"

Cadence shook his head with a smirk.

Chapter 6
Second Dagger

Three a.m., Ten Days Later

Cadence walked carefully through the darkness holding his sword Ethereal in one hand and his revolver in the other. He heard shadow demons scurrying across the floors and walls, but he couldn't see them. Shadow demons are made of moving shadows and were considered the scum of the dark, the lowest demons scraped from the bottom of a shoe. They were small pitch-black creatures, their skin tightly stretched around their bones; the head was too large for their bodies. The eyes were sunk deep back behind the dark, with veins that glowed a red fog around them. The teeth were white and razor-sharp, with the front two longer than the rest, like a vampire. The first one jumped at Cadence; he pointed his revolver, squeezed the trigger as the bullet slammed into the demon's head as it flew back and slapped against the darkness with a wet sticky sound. He twirled his sword in his hand in a circular motion over and over the demons, with black gooey blood splattering everywhere, all over the dark walls and floor. Cadence must have killed over a hundred demons when he heard a faint echoey sound like a phone ringing.

"Huh?" He turned to look behind him into the darkness: there was a faint light. He looked back at the dead limbs and innards scattered everywhere. "You are all going back to hell where you belong." Cadence turned and walked toward the light and reached for the phone.

"Hello? Huh, who is this?" Cadence breathed in, coming out of a deep sleep. He ran his hands through his slept-in hair. "Who is this again?"

"Lieutenant Anne Black. I need you to come down here now."

"What — now?" He was feeling a little groggy from fighting and killing demons through the night while he slept; oh, and the few bottles of wine he'd had before he went to bed.

"We have another one of those weird dagger murders. What did you call it — The Eyes of Coals?"

"OK, OK, I'm getting up." His top lip stuck to his teeth; he felt crappy, like a wiffleball bat had smacked him square in the face.

"Give me twenty minutes. Oh, and by the way — it's called The Eyes for the Souls. Shit! Why doesn't anyone listen anymore?" Cadence got out of bed, walked over to the bathroom, turned on the light, looked in the mirror, and splashed cold water on his face to wake himself up. He sat there thinking about the dagger. How did it link to him and the blue-purple flame?

Heather said I would meet him soon. How does she know that? When and where will this take place?

Cadence softly sighed, then rubbed his hand across his chin, turned, and started the shower. He was a little excited to go meet up with Anne while further investigating the dagger.

***

"Hey Anne — all right? What do we have?" Cadence asked, rubbing his hands together in a quick motion. They were behind the Orleans Casino on Cameron Street. The girl's body was behind bushes in a small dark nook of the building. The poor girl's eyes were missing, and she had bite marks on her arms. They overlapped the cut marks that started from her hands and worked their way up to her shoulders.

"This girl's death differs from the first, except for the dagger in the chest. This one seems more… personal. What a mess. Does this mean anything to you?" Anne asked.

Cadence stroked his chin and then rubbed his cheek. "It's different because it's the second witch, Kaliea. She is not one to mess with; she's powerful." Cadence looked over at Anne. She had a slightly confused look on her face.

"OK, now there's another witch?" Anne asked.

"Well, let's have a look at this dagger, shall we?" Cadence bent down and cocked his head around the dagger's side, just in time to witness the blood flow up the second etched line and move toward the second skull on the handle.

Cadence went to grab the hilt of the dagger and pull it free from the bloody chest, but he quickly pulled his hand back as if a lightning bolt had stabbed it.

"Shit!" Cadence yelped. "That's not good. Why didn't you call me sooner with this?"

"Really? Really?" Anne barked back.

"The second witch is nearby, and I'm not talking about miles away. I think she is here."

The dagger moved as it slowly slid up and pulled out of the dead girl's chest, then following was the tightly snuggled skin sealed around the blade. The dagger floated in the air, then turned so it was horizontal and pointed toward Cadence. It pulled back and darted in a straight line. Cadence moved his head slightly to the right and the dagger sliced across his left cheekbone, skin ripping open. The first layer of skin widened; red meat showed, and blood formed around the open wound. The dagger slammed into the wall behind him with a loud twang, moving back and forth.

"Shit! Are you all right?" yelled Anne, with a hint of concern in her voice. The dagger wiggled and pulled free from the wall, turned, and darted through the crowd, parting bystanders throwing themselves out of the way. Then it disappeared into the distance.

"Yeah, yeah — I'm fine."

"Shit, tell me you saw that."

"Yeah, I did. The witch called it back to her."

"So, I'm guessing that is the same dagger from the first murder," said Anne.

"This dagger is dangerous, and yes, it's the same dagger."

"My God, how old do you think it is?"

"I'm thinking thousands of years."

"Thousands!" Anne's eyes lit up.

"I've seen this dagger before, over a hundred years ago, being pulled from a body. I thought nothing of it. It's scaring the hell out of me because I don't know what they're using it for."

Anne stared at Cadence with a peculiar look.

"A hundred years ago, huh? What do you think you are, immortal or something?" She threw her head back and laughed.

"Yeah, something like that."

Anne's smile disappeared as she handed Cadence a cloth to put on his cheek to control the bleeding. "Wow, I thought you were a little strange, Cadence. Now I believe you are a lot of strange."

***

Year 1824

Cadence was lying on his back in bed with Meadow, the youngest of the three witches, on top, pumping slowly up and down, then faster, and wet — very wet. His hands found her breasts. Sweat glistened off them, leaving a beautiful sight that any man would have wished they could lay eyes on. Her head snapped back as Cadence released inside of her. She fell on top of him, exhausted, panting, and sweating.

"My god, that was amazing."

The room was large, and everything in the place was white: the walls, bed, sheets, all the furniture, and the floor was white marble. The doors that were open and led to the balcony, letting in a slight breeze coming in from the morning air, were white.

Cadence and Meadow had been in love for a little more than a year. They still had not told her father, but the two older sisters did not sit well with their younger sister's love choices. The oldest, Kaliea, was always a pain in the ass. Cadence never knew, only suspected, that they were witches, who would haunt his brother and him to this very day.

The door burst open, and Meadow flew over the side of the bed.

"What the hell? What the hell is going on here?" Kaliea yelled. "You need to get your priorities straight, girl; he is a low-class peasant."

"Get the hell out!" Meadow yelled, wrapping the blanket around her naked body. "You and Heather, you are both assholes; why can't you leave us alone. Why do you try to pry between us all the time?"

"Well, let me explain, bitch! He is not who you think he is." Kaliea threw both hands forward. Thin blue lightning shot out and hit Meadow, sending her back against the wall. Cadence stared with his mouth open, not knowing what to do or say.

"I'm sorry, I'm sorry!" Meadow's eyes were panic-stricken. Cadence turned toward Kaliea. He wanted to kill her right where she stood. Kaliea glared over at him with an evil smile pasted to her face.

"Get the fuck out!" Meadow screamed as white-blue lightning flickered on and off around her body.

There was a quick, small glint in Kaliea's eyes as fear set in, and then black-gray smoke hit the room as Kaliea disappeared. Meadow ran over to Cadence and buried herself in his arms.

***

"What is this place? It's the second time you have brought me here," Anne said.

"You brought her here to the room, and you didn't tell her?" Jenny said. "Whoa-ho! I love it; I have to see this."

"Please, Jenny, don't you need to lock up the store or dust off some items up front, maybe go to the bathroom? You know, something like that."

"Oh, hell, no!" A little snort came from Jenny. "I don't want to miss this." She stared at Cadence; his eyes darted toward the door.

"OK, OK, I get the hint. I'm out of here." Jenny walked backward, enjoying every step she took. "Are you going to show her your trick?" she asked with a snort and an evil smile forming on her face.

"Shut up and go!" Cadence had anger with an amused look on his face and a little shaky twitch in his right eye.

"So, what trick are you going to show me?"

"Really — it's nothing."

"Why am I getting the feeling you are holding something back from me." Anne enjoyed the mystery game Cadence was playing; she thought it was cute and charming.

Anne broke the silence first. "OK, let's get started. There have been two girls stabbed and killed with the same dagger," she said, "that's called Lies with the Souls." Anne giggled. A heavy playful sigh came with the rolling of Cadence's eyes.

"That's The Eyes for the Souls, dammit!" Cadence bent backward. He could feel his spine cracking and popping, with his arms stretched out.

"Ugh! What the hell?" Cadence screamed.

"Cade! Are you all right? What's happening?"

"You killed my dear sweet sister, and now it's your turn. You will die soon, oh, and brutal it will be."

"Kaliea!" Cadence screamed. He saw her in a dark cloak, her face hidden by a hood in heavy shadows, with a sudden, loud, reverse sound to her voice.

"You will die soon!"

Anne grabbed Cadence by his arm with a shake. "Hey! Snap out of it — Earth to Cade."

Cadence snapped back. "What the hell happened? Shit, I wanted to show you something, and then — that happened." He shook his head to pull himself back to reality. "I wanted to show you, so you can understand what is going on."

"What the hell? Why do you keep bending back like that? I have to say you're kind of freaking me out."

"Do you think I like it? To answer your question, it's how the witches are communicating with me."

"By bending you back like that? You would think there would be an easier way." Anne looked over at the wall of swords. "Oh, my god! This sword! It's a *Koto Period Tachi sword*, with a curved blade; this is about four hundred to five hundred years old."

"They have shortened the blade through the years," Cadence said. "That's a favorite of mine. You know your swords."

"Where did you get all this amazing stuff?"

"I've collected things over the years."

"Well, I can see you collect wonderful things. Is this the revolver from Hitler's hand, the one he shot himself in the head with in 1945?" Anne's face was gleaming with joy.

"Yes, now please put the revolver down — ah, carefully — that's worth a lot of money. Now you are freaking *me* out. You seem way too excited about this stuff."

"So, what are you going to show me?"

Cadence ignored her question. "Now, the dagger has three heads on the handle, and twice the blood streamed up to two of the heads. So, what will happen when blood reaches the third skull?"

"Do we want to find out?" Anne said. "So, Cade, what do you want to show me? And please, stop changing the subject…"

Chapter 7
Little Jenny

There was a scream. "Aaahhh!" It was ear-piercing, and Kaliea, the second witch, appeared. She seemed thin and sickly, like she had not eaten for months. Her hair was long, straight, and scraggly looking, with the scalp showing through. Her eyes were sunk deep in her skull, and her skin was very pale, as if she had lived in a dark cave for years. Her gown was long, torn, and dirty, dragging behind her. Then she disappeared. Silence, then she reappeared: "Eccchh!" And she disappeared again.

"OK, now what the hell was that?" Anne asked, her face worried, mouth open. "It just keeps getting weirder," she said.

"I promise you will understand pain. I will come for you for what you have done to my sister."

"Who the hell is that?" Anne yelled, frantically looking around. Her Glock was in both hands, pointing at nothing dancing around in the shadows.

"She's gone, all right? She's gone; don't be frightened," Cadence said.

"I'm not scared. I just want to know who the hell that was. OK, I'm a little scared. Now can you please just tell me what is going on?"

"All right, calm down," Cadence said.

"I want to understand what is going on, that's all. Why should I calm down?" Anne put her arms around herself; she was shaking and cold. They heard another scream, but this time the sound came from upstairs inside the store.

"Jenny!" Cadence bolted up the stairs, taking two steps at a time until he reached the top. "Jenny, I'm coming!" Cadence screamed again.

With a hard, quick kick to the door, next to the knob, the door splintered and gave way. It flew open, slamming against the wall.

"Jenny, I'm here!" He entered the room, Anne right behind him with her Glock in hand. She looked at Cadence first, and then she followed Cadence's stare. Her eyes went wide as she gazed toward the ceiling. She saw Jenny just floating at the ceiling with shadows moving all around her.

"Let — her — go!" Cadence yelled. There was a loud crackling noise, a heavy wind not blowing, but pulling, sucking. In seconds, half of Jenny's body became engulfed by the sucking wind.

"Uncle Cade! Please help me! It hurts, oh my god, it hurts," she screamed.

"You mother-fucking bitch! Kaliea, let her go!" Cadence yelled out.

"Oh, Cade — this is only the beginning of the pain. Do you like it?"

Cadence ran toward Jenny and grabbed her hand. "I've got you, Jenny; hold on to me."

Kaliea threw both arms forward. A force of lightning flew straight at Cadence, hitting him in the chest. Cadence flew against the wall with a loud thud! Pain shot through Cadence's upper body. His head snapped back, as he screamed in pain. He looked down; blood squirted past a splintered wood shard protruding from the wall. A clump of meat from his chest hung from the end of the splinter. Cadence coughed once, twice; a blood bubble formed on his lips.

"Shit!" Anne screamed. "Cade! Holy shit!"

They both heard Jenny pleading and turned their heads in her direction.

"Uncle Cade, help me!"

Cadence screamed, "Aaaaggghhh!" Arms flew behind him. Palms hit flat against the wall. Cadence pushed — Aggh!— Pushed harder — anger — pushed — anger turned to rage, rage into hate.

"LET—HER—GO NOW!"

The spike slowly slid back through his chest and muscle. The meat at the tip of the splinter fell off, hitting the floor with a loud wet smack! Blood splashed his shoe.

Anne stood there, eyes wide, mouth open, breathing very shallow. Her lips silently mouthed the words: *"What the hell!"*

Cadence fell to his knees, head down, exhausted, and feeling unbearable pain. "LET—HER—GO!" he screamed again. Right then, his head snapped back, eyes glowing blue-green, and his fingers spread as they shot straight out. Cadence stood with his arms stretched out. Different colors shot out from his fingertips, and everything seemed like time had slowed down. Cadence flashed like he was double, back and forth like a bad VHS video, warping and doubling like there were two of him. All Cadence could hear was David Bowie's *Heroes*, like he was floating with the dolphins. His green eyes darted toward Kaliea.

The room lit up; Cadence cried out. The room lit up even brighter, and Kaliea's eyes widened. She didn't know Cadence could harness that much energy.

Jenny screamed! "It hurts!" Tears were streaming down Jenny's cheeks.

Cadence grabbed for Jenny, but then she was jerked back into the sucking wind. And then she was gone. The sucking wind, the light, shadows, Jenny, and Kaliea — they were all gone.

It was an empty room except for Cadence and Anne just standing there. Her mouth was open and pale, as if she had just seen a ghost. The energy and colorful glowing light surrounding Cadence disappeared.

"What just happened?" She glowered at Cadence.

"She's gone. Yeah, she's gone." Sweat was dripping down; as a drop hit the ground, the splash vibrated through the room. Cadence looked down. Anne looked over at Cadence; he appeared beaten and tired.

"What the hell is that on the back of your neck?" Anne noticed something moving on his neck.

"Wha—what?" Cadence grabbed the back of his neck and felt a loose, meaty lump. He didn't have time to worry about it.

"Shit, Jenny," Cadence whispered.

"*I will find you. Oh, trust me, I will find you.*"

Cadence jumped up and ran for the secret room, not caring that Anne was right behind him. He moved the skull's eye and pushed the button; the stairs fell into place.

"Cade! Cade!" Anne yelled after him. "Stop! Can you please tell me what the hell is going on?" She stopped at the entrance, looked over at the skull head, then passed the door and stared into the darkness and whispered to herself, "*What the hell did I get myself into?*"

"Anne, leave me alone. I have to figure out how to get Jenny back before Kaliea keeps her promise and kills her. I need to think."

Cadence grabbed a book off the shelf, brought it over to the podium, and slammed it on the flat surface. Cadence started rapidly flipping through the pages, looking for an answer there was no question to.

"The bitch will pay!" He picked the book up and slammed it down again. "Fuck!"

Calmly, Anne touched Cadence's arm. "Can you please explain what's going on here? Maybe I can help. I'm all confused. You should be lying in the morgue, but you're not dead, you're still here. Why?"

"Never mind me, we need to find Jenny! I need to get her back. Shit! Shit!"

"Stop it! How are you still alive? Tell me." Anne calmly grabbed Cadence's hand.

"Hey, guys! What's up!" came a voice from the entrance to the room. Cadence and Anne turned swiftly toward the source of the voice. His face was bruised, with two front teeth missing, one eye closed completely, and a big smile showing through all of it. He looked comical.

"Come on, Cade, it's me — it's Tom!"

Chapter 8
The Return of Tom Jones

"Who is she? And why is she here in our secret room?" Tom asked, annoyed at the situation he had walked in on.

"Tom, this is Lieutenant Anne Black, and she is here in *my* secret room."

Tom folded his arms across his chest. The cast on his arm seemed awkward and painful to him.

"Anne has seen strange things lately and heard the bumps in the night. So, I have to explain all the weird things and all the bumps she's freaked out about. She needs to understand my world."

"Listen, Cadsie, are you sure about this? I think you are making a big mistake. All I mean is, can we trust her?"

"Tom! Stop." Cadence showed some annoyance on his face. He sighed and ran his fingers through his hair and calmed himself down. "She has every right to know the truth, and besides, we will need all the help we can get."

"Yeah, sure. Help for what?" Tom said, confused.

"Well, a witch bitch came here for revenge on me. Instead, she took Jenny from us. The witch knows I'll come for her to get her back."

"Oh, no! Our little Jenny?" Tom showed a concerned look on his face. "When did this happen?"

"Just minutes ago," Anne barked. "So, can we please hurry up with this? The sooner you explain, the quicker we can understand how to bring Jenny back to us and figure out what this dagger is for."

"OK, Anne, this is it. Here is my story." Cadence explained the year he was born, followed with how and when he discovered his immortality, and how his mother disappeared after talking with a blue-purple flame. Then he gave the history of the three witches, who they were and how he had to keep moving from place to place through the centuries to avoid this very conflict. All the while, Anne just stood there, her mouth and eyes wide open in disbelief.

"You know," Anne said, "if I hadn't seen all this shit myself firsthand, I would turn you around, slam you against that wall, slap cuffs on you so fast, and bring you straight to the psycho ward. But all I keep hearing is that poor Jenny floating in the air and screaming how it hurt. So — I'm in. What do we do next?"

"Well, I'm researching what happens to the dagger and what the third skull will do after stabbing the next young girl; this will be the key to finding my niece. Tom, can you go through these books and gather information for me? I hope something here will give us some history on this dagger. I will take Anne with me. I need to dig up an old friend." Cadence set a stack of books on the table in front of Tom.

"Cade! No, that's not a good idea. I'm asking you — don't do this."

"Tom, I have to do this. He is the only one that can help us. There will be no discussion over this; so, please, search the books, find some useful information. Oh! Shit! I'm sorry, I forgot to ask, how are you feeling?"

"Like a fucking witch bitch beat the hell out of me."

"Did you get a positive look at her?"

"Shit, I don't know, and I don't think I want to know. I'm a little embarrassed that it was a girl who did this to me."

"Here, check out this picture of three girls who I think may have done this to you. Can you point out the one that slapped you around?"

Tom stared at Cadence. "Really? Jeez!" Tom shook his head.

"A little sensitive, are we?" Cadence's finger tapped on the picture. "This is Kaliea. That's her, right?"

"No, no, that's her right there." Tom's finger landed on the face of the witch who beat him up in his apartment. Cadence stared at the photo. His head cocked slightly, with confused thinking stuck to his face.

"Cade — everything all right?" Anne said.

"Yeah, just…"

"Well, what's wrong?" Anne asked.

"That's not Kaliea."

"Then who is it?" Tom barked.

"Heather, her name is Heather."

"Isn't that the girl you killed at the bar?" Anne folded her arms in front of her.

"Wait, you mean you killed this girl — really?" Tom asked, surprised at this.

"Yeah, I did, Tom. Shit, I don't know why I didn't think of her. I should've realized. I know she could be ruthless, but not like her sister Kaliea."

"Oh, my," Tom stared at the picture again.

"What's wrong, Tom? Do you recognize one of them?" Cadence asked, following Tom's gaze.

"That one there, she's the blonde one — she was there. She stopped the bitch from kicking my face in."

"What, her? I didn't even know she was back?" Cadence rubbed his chin while thinking. "Why didn't Meadow come to me with this?"

"Why would she come to see you?" Tom looked at Cadence.

"We have some history between us. I don't understand; Meadow is not working with her sisters or with this dagger game. Why?" Cadence straightened up and breathed in, confused, and tried to make some sense of all this. He shook his head to bring himself back to the conversation in the room.

"Well, who is she?" Tom asked.

"Her name is Meadow. She is the youngest of the sisters. She was the weakest of the three, but her father believed that she would be more powerful in time than both the others.”

“So, what happened?” Anne was now showing interest in this weirdness around her.

“She disappeared, but that’s a story for another day. Let’s go, Anne. Tom, can you start reading the book? Are you sure you’re all right, Tom? You don’t look so good.”

Tom seemed tired and confused. “Yeah, I hurt a little; my right eye is puffy and black, and it stings like hell. Oh, and my broken teeth make me jump a little when I breathe in and the air hits the nerve — it’s a fun sensation. Yeah! It fucking hurts! What kind of question is—?”

“Well, I’m sorry to hear that. I hope you feel better soon,” Cadence interrupted with a chuckle as he walked out the door at the front of the store.

“Come on, Anne. Let’s go dig someone up and have some fun.”

“Hahaha, you are something else, Cadence,” Anne said.

“Yeah, well, if you want to be amused, poison me, stab me, shoot me, but not in the head — that hurts like a bitch. Now, Anne, take my hand.”

Anne reluctantly grabbed Cadence’s hand. Her head flew back as the visions of another place with an old park in ruins flashed through her head. Blood ran through their noses, eyes, and ears. Time slowed; Anne smelled honey and almonds. They were standing in an old park that had been there for hundreds of years, with no one around.

"Well, we're here," Cadence said with a smile on his lips.

Chapter 9
Sam Locke

"All right, where are we? Why isn't anyone here? Cadence, how did we get here? Oh, wait, are we able to get back? We're not stuck here, are we? I'm feeling a little nauseous." Anne bent over and threw up.

Cadence let out a sarcastic laugh. "I have to say, I think I should have brought Tom with me and left you to search through the books. Jeez. Well, to answer some of your *many* questions, his name is Sam. He is older than me by three hundred years, and yes, we are almost at our destination."

"You mean there are more like you?" Anne asked, staring at Cadence, shaking her head and wiping her mouth. "OK, how did we get here?"

"It's harder than you think to do what I just did."

"What did you just do?" Anne asked sarcastically.

"As for your other question. Yes, there are more like me. Sam took me under his wing. He practically raised Christopher and me; he found us after our mother disappeared. We were starving and cold in an old, abandoned church just outside Nice, France, here in this town, Peillon. He took us into his home with his daughters, fed and clothed us. He educated us, taught us of the world, and the evil that surrounded it. He is the one that taught and trained me in the dark magic I possess."

"Well, what happened to him?"

"Oh… well… you know, I used my magic and froze him in a wall."

Anne turned her head to look at Cadence. The cop in her wanted to arrest him, but all she could say was, "Oh! Well, that explains the expression on Tom's face."

They walked a little bit further through the old park until Cadence saw the wall.

"There!" Cadence pointed to a brick wall; they walked up to an old, burned-down public bath and shower facility somewhere at the edge of Peillon. There were only two walls of masonry brick blocks left standing through the years. Cadence walked over and held up a sledgehammer as he heard Pink Floyd's *Another Brick in the Wall* in his head. He swung the hammer and hit the first brick.

Forty-five minutes later, the wall finally gave.

"Wow! I can see you work out." Anne chuckled at what she had said. Sweat was dripping down Cadence's face.

"You are a blast of fresh air, you know that."

Anne looked over at the rubble. She saw a hand, stiff and straight, sticking out of the masonry wall.

"What the hell is that, and is it moving?"

Slowly, a finger twitched, then a second finger moved. The hand formed a fist and pulled back under the masonry rubble. Then, with a loud burst, the hand shot up through the masonry wall. With an explosion, rock and debris shot out in all directions. The dust that surrounded them was wet from the blood in the air. A shape of an outlined body was lying face down on the ground, slowly standing up — a hulk of a man. His hair was black and hung down past his shoulders. He had a scar straight across his forehead to his temple, down the side of his jaw and back across, slicing each corner of his mouth. He was sporting a beard due to his time spent inside the wall. Sam looked around at the decayed park where he had last stood. He breathed in the cool night air.

"Hey Cady, so, what year is it?" Sam looked around, taking in the scenery. His bones hurt, and his joints were stiff.

"Sam," Cadence nervously said. "So — how have you been?"

Anne snorted and turned away.

"Well, you know, I'm a little cold and stiff here and there, Cade. So, before I tear you apart into little bloody pieces, care to explain why you put me in that wall?"

"Well, let's see. You were way out of control back in 1831. I had to stop you before innocent people got hurt. I protected you, and I would do it again if it saved you, your daughter, and all those innocent people from harm."

***

Sam was sitting down on a park bench, head down, resting in both hands. Cadence and Christopher were sitting beside him.

"No, no," he said calmly to himself. "Why? Why did she do this? She could not control her powers. Leah should never have let her use them without me there to supervise."

"Sam, we understand your pain. We're sorry this happened," Christopher said.

Sam glared up without moving his head. Evilness spread across his face. His upper lip curled back, exposing his teeth, as the shadows danced around him.

"You know nothing of my pain!" Sam growled. "So, stop pretending you do. My little girl killed her mother. My youngest baby just killed my wife!"

Sam stood up, white lightning spreading through his fingers, like spider webs through each one, making his hands deadly.

"Sam?" Cadence asked. "What's happening, what are you doing?"

"My little innocent Meadow; why, how did this happen?"

Sam's head snapped back. White lightning swirled around his body, whiter than they'd ever seen before, until you couldn't see his body, but only an outline, forming a lot of rage.

Christopher ran toward Sam. "Sam, stop, what are you doing?" he screamed. "There are families here."

"Both of you back up; don't come near me. I will disintegrate you where you stand."

"Cadence!" Christopher yelled. "Move out of the way."

"No! I will not," Cadence said, standing between Christopher and Sam.

"Christopher, please, he's been like a father to us. He took us into his home, for God's sake."

A heavy wind mixed with lightning hit Christopher and sent him across the park, slamming him into a tree and breaking his arm. Bark flew everywhere.

"No!" Cadence screamed. "Why would you do that to Christopher? Sam, you need to stop this!" He ran over to make sure his brother was OK.

"Christopher…"

"I'm fine, Cade," his brother cut him off abruptly. "Make sure Sam doesn't hurt anyone."

Cadence stood and faced Sam. "Sam, that's enough — there are too many people here. Kids and parents are in harm's way. Stop this madness. Think of what you are doing."

Sam's hands shot down toward the ground. His fingers spread, all building up more lightning, as he screamed his wife's name. "LEAH! MY LEAH!"

Mothers and fathers grabbed their kids, running; dogs barked while backing up. Sam's eyes turned white, his pupils a large evil black. Christopher shook and was lifted off the ground. Cadence took a stand, ready for Sam.

"You were always a pain in the ass, Christopher, not like your brother here. Cadence is good; he listens, he obeys. Cade is a better student with the dark magic than you ever were — hell, Cade is even better than my daughters; he just doesn't know it yet."

Christopher screamed at hearing this, but could not move.

"Sam, stop this madness!" Cadence said.

Christopher pulled forward, suspended in the air while holding his arm, then slammed hard against a brick wall of the park's structure. Cadence raised his hands in front and shot a thin line of lightning at Sam.

"Sam, stop, please," he pleaded. Sam laughed at the sparkle that hit him and fizzled out.

"Cady, when did you learn that? Never mind. That high school magic will not hurt me."

Cadence stepped to the right, dodging Sam's retaliation, sending a burst into the brick wall behind him. Exploding pieces spread all around him. Cadence looked up and sent a lightning bolt to hit a branch from the tree above Sam's head. Sam looked up to see the tree branch falling; Cadence ran toward him, screaming. Holding the amulet that Meadow made for him in his hand, he wrapped his arms around Sam. As they hit the brick wall, Cadence pushed Sam and threw himself backward in the other direction, eyes shut hard. Simultaneously, the brick wall opened up and engulfed

Sam and froze him instantly inside. Then the light faded.

"Christopher, are you OK?"

"Yeah, I'm fine." Christopher stood and dusted himself off, favoring his broken arm. "I guess you've been practicing there, little brother."

"Every chance I get. I think I am getting the hang of it."

"What did you do with Sam?" Christopher pointed over in the wall's direction. "You able to get him back?"

"I didn't think it through yet. Give me some time. I'll figure it out." Cadence looked over at the wall and thought to himself, *What the hell did I just do?*

Chapter 10
Jenny's Return

"So — you're saying that Sam here is the father of the three witches trying to kill you?" Anne asked as they waited for Sam to adjust to his surroundings and how old the park looked.

"Anne, listen, he can help us. He doesn't know what's going on yet. When we bring him up to speed, I know he will help us get Jenny back."

A heavy sigh escaped Sam's lungs. "Cady, you still haven't told me what year it is."

"It's 2019; sorry, Sam, I'm not ignoring you. I have a lot on my mind, and I need your help to figure these issues out."

"OK, but first tell me how you did that trick, melting me into the wall?"

Cadence put a crooked smile on his face and turned to Sam. "Well, Sam, it was an old high school trick."

Sam snickered at the comment. "I guess I deserve that. So, tell me, Cade, why did you free me from the wall? You need something from me, don't you?"

"I'll explain everything to you, but for now, we need to get you back to the store."

"I'm not looking forward to this, Cade," Anne said.

"I know, but take my hand anyway, Anne." Cadence wore a smile.

***

The door to the store swung open.

"Tom! Where are you?"

"Yeah, yeah, I'm back here," Tom cried out.

"Hey Tom, I want to introduce you to Sam."

"You mean *the* Sam?" Tom said with a hint of sarcasm in his voice. "You know, Cade here has talked a lot about you. It's a pleasure to meet a real living legend."

"Yeah, I don't know about this legend thing, but I do smell like something died. I've spent a hundred and eighty-eight years frozen in a brick wall, and I could use a nice bath." Sam glanced over at Cadence.

Tom scrunched his nose and motioned his hand to follow him. "Yep, come with me. You can use the shower to clean up. I'll gather up some clothes for you to wear. I hope I can find some that will fit; you're a big man." Sam stood there and stared at the shower, looking at it up and down.

"Yeah, right, you don't know what a modern shower looks like," Tom said out loud while standing next to Sam.

"So, this is a shower?" Sam poked his head inside. "How does it work?"

81

"Here, let me turn it on for you." Tom reached over and turned the water on and set it to warm. Steam rose. Sam put his hand under the streaming water.

"How is this hot? You don't have to boil the water first?"

"Nope, just turn the little handle and *voilà* — hot water," Tom said.

"Well, isn't that something. I like it." Sam smiled and removed his towel, standing there naked. Tom spun to avoid looking at Sam in his birthday suit.

"All right, seen too much." Tom turned, embarrassed, and left the bathroom.

***

"Oh my! That was wonderful." Sam walked into Cadence's office, where everyone was gathered. "That had to be the second most amazing feeling I ever had. A shower after a hundred and eighty-eight years — and without waiting for the water to boil, no less." Sam grinned from ear to ear.

"I have to ask," Tom said. "What was the first wonderful…"

"Tom!" Cadence snapped. "Please let's focus on finding Jenny!"

"Oh, oh! Right. Yes, here's what I have so far. They used a banishing spell. It's a spell done in reverse." Sam's voice overlapped Tom's, giving a stereo effect. "It's a reverse spell that creates a vortex that pulls whoever they cast upon and sucks them right into it," Tom continued the explanation.

"So how do we reverse this vortex spell?" Cadence asked.

"Well, this is my oldest daughter we are talking about here, right?" Sam said. "It will be challenging for us, and I have been out of the game for a while — like a few hundred years, give or take a little, no thanks to Cade here."

"Again, I'm sorry about that, Sam." Cadence looked toward the ground, not making eye contact with him.

"Why is she so quiet? Haven't heard a peep out of her since we got here." Sam thumbed over toward Anne.

Anne looked up. "Me? I am still trying to wrap my head around this entire thing. I need to get some sleep and process this — whatever *this* is. I… just… never mind. I have to go." Anne walked fast toward the door and stepped outside.

"Wait! Anne!" Cadence ran after her. Anne stopped and faced Cadence. "Hey, are you all right, Anne?"

"No, Cade, I'm not; I just need to get some sleep to process this."

"I'll call you tomorrow, OK?" Cadence said. He looked worried for Anne and how she was taking this all in.

Anne shrugged her shoulders. "Yeah sure, you know — Saturday, it's my day off."

"Great," said Cadence. "I will call you tomorrow, we'll talk then."

"Sure, sounds good," Anne disappeared down the street.

***

"HELLO! ANYONE! CAN ANYONE HEAR ME?" Her screams seemed to come from inside the stone walls. The room was dark and damp, and the stone walls had water trickling down in various areas. The ceiling was high and created echoes when she yelled out. Jenny slumped down against the wall and put her head on her knees, feeling cold and scared.

"Uncle Cade, where are you?"

***

Anne sat at the edge of her bed, half-naked. Steam from the shower had been rolling into the room for the last twenty minutes. Her arms were folded around her body. She was trying to make sense out of the previous twenty-four hours she had experienced. She stood up slowly. Her long, beautiful legs walked to the bathroom. She pulled her T-shirt off and stepped into the shower, putting her head under the hot water with steam rising all around her. She put her head back under the water and sighed. After ten minutes, she turned off the water. She grabbed the towel from the hook, dried off, and wrapped the towel around her body. She sat back down at the edge of her bed, still confused about everything. Laying back, she fell into a deep sleep.

"Anne… Anne…" The voice flowed toward her with far-away soft echoes. *"It's mommy!"*

Anne sat up, extending her arms out. "Mommy?" Tears were falling down her cheeks. "Why?"

Her mom moved forward! She stopped in front of Anne. *"WHY? BECAUSE YOU STOPPED BELIEVING!"*

Anne sat straight up, panting uncontrollably, with sweat pouring down her face. "Mommy!" Ever since her mother had died from cancer two years earlier, the nightmares kept coming more often; she couldn't seem to control them.

***

Year 2017

Anne's mom told her she had lung cancer. It was aggressive, she would not live to see the end of the year. Anne fell into darkness and retreated away from everyone and everything around her. Her mother was very religious, but Anne did not believe in God. She cursed God; he was taking her mother from her too soon and in such a cruel and painful way. Since she was a little girl, Anne had not stepped into a church.

Anne was by her mother's side when she passed away. The last breath her mother spoke to her was, *"What made you stop believing?"*

***

Present Day

"Hello my child," whispered a soft, slimy sound of a voice.

"Who's there?" Jenny said with a little quiver in her voice.

"Do you know why you are here?"

"What? Why I'm here?" She looked all around the dark as the voice bounced from wall to wall.

"Do you know why you are here?" the voice calmly asked again. *"Someone you know did something terrible. So, I will ask you again: do you know why you are here?"* The voice screamed this time.

"I… I don't know why I am here," sniffled Jenny.

There came a sickly laugh with a lot of phlegm dancing around in its throat. *"Hahaha"* the evil laugh trailed off. *"Cadence killed my sister."*

"My uncle will come for me, and when he does, well — you will be sorry," Jenny said. She felt ridiculous saying that. *Jeez, I can't believe I just said that.*

"You already tried to kill my uncle once, and you failed!" Jenny yelled again. "What is wrong with you and your sisters anyway, and where the fuck am I?"

"I will take Cadence's blood from him while slicing into his flesh," the sickly voice said. *"Oh, and what a delicious moment that will be."*

The door opened and in walked a man, around seven to eight feet tall. His face was hidden by the shadows dancing around him. His hair was long and scraggly, dirty, with wetness dripping from the ends. His eyes had a slight dark reddening to them, and his fingers were long and bony, with long and sharp nails protruding from the ends of each finger.

Jenny gagged from the smell as bile formed at the top of her throat. His voice was almost a hissing whisper.

"So — you're Cadence Mage's niece, eh? The fun we will have, little Jenny."

The tall man's hand shot out, his long fingers and the nails at the ends slid just under Jenny's ribcage with a soft squishy sound; he was searching for her soul. Jenny screamed out in agony. A low, deep laugh was bellowing up from the throat of the tall man.

"My… uncle… will come for you," Jenny painfully said.

"Oh, you sweet, naïve, beautiful child. That pain you are experiencing is your soul being penetrated. The pain will only get worse. Then Cadence will hear your pleading cries. Oh, and then I will take pleasure in

meeting your uncle." The tall man dug his nails further into Jenny's soul. She screamed louder, her echoes bouncing off the stone walls. The tall man quickly looked up into Jenny's eyes with fear on his face.

"You... I can't believe... you are the one. You are the darkness. Who are you?" The slow hissing whisper of the tall man shook with fright. The tall man pulled away and backed up next to Kaliea.

"She is special. She will be the one," he whispered.

Kaliea looked over at Jenny with disgust on her face. *"I fucking hate her."*

***

Saturday (Anne's Day Off)

"Cadence!" Anne cried out. "Wait, can you please slow down?"

"Come on! Hurry, we have to get to the center of the city, and we're almost there." Cadence kept walking at a fast pace.

"Why?" Anne tried to keep up.

"Because I need you to kill me."

"What? Be serious, and why in the center of the city?"

"Why? The center is where Sam's daughter's magic is pulling from the strongest, and if I die in this section of the city, it should be long enough to see Jenny, grab her, and pull her back through the vortex." Cadence went to turn around. "Now, Anne."

Right then, a bullet went soaring through his brain with a sickening crack of Cadence's skull. He stepped back. He was staring dead straight at Anne with bewilderment on his face, and with a gurgling bloody whisper, "*Good one!*"

***

"Uncle Cade! Please help me — where are you? Please, I hope you are coming for me." Jenny looked around and saw three black creatures darting across the walls and ceiling all around her. They were up at the ceiling, then scurrying down by the floor, running through each other. She was scared and cried out to her uncle again.

"*I'm here, Jenny*," came a whisper from Cadence's lips next to her ear. His face appeared out of the darkness. Jenny gasped. Her head snapped to one side. "*I'm getting you the hell out of here.*"

"*Uncle Cadence…*" A long gurgling laugh sounded in front of Jenny, hidden by the shadows. "*So — you think you can save her?*" Kaliea laughed again.

"*Well, I'm sure I can. See — I'm dead. I am in the dream world. You can't touch me, so shut the hell up, you ugly bitch. Jenny, take my hand. I'm taking you home. When we get back, give me about ten minutes, and don't… freak out on me.*"

Jenny stretched out her quivering hand.

"WHO THE FUCK? WHO HELPED YOU?" Kaliea yelled.

A white-blue lightning crackling noise moved through the air. The tall man appeared in front of Cadence, black slime dripping down from the center of his bottom lip.

"So — you're Cadence Mage. You don't look dangerous."

"Yeah, well, I never claimed to be, asshole."

***

Year 1821

The demon hunter dropped to his knees with blood and spit drooling down from his bottom lip until it broke off and slapped the ground. He whispered to the demon standing in front of him.

"The next demon hunter will come for you and send you back to hell." The demon, named Egran, laughed while he watched the demon hunter take his last breath and fall forward. His hand loosened as the sword dropped and clanked noisily to the ground. The demon Egran reached down and pulled the large sword from the hunter's torso and swiped the flat part of the blade across his tongue, savoring the metallic-tasting blood that lay on his taste buds, and then he swallowed, with a bellowed raspy voice.

"I'm looking forward to it, hunter, I'm looking forward to it."

When Cadence fell asleep, he found himself walking through darkness. He kept walking until he came across a light shining down on a corpse kneeling with its head down. As Cadence stood next to the fallen demon hunter, he noticed a sword lying next him, reached for it and held it up in front of his face. He noticed on the blade next to the guard the inscription read *Ethereal*. Egran slowly rose behind Cadence; the demon was large.

"So, you are the new demon hunter, ha, ha! They sent a boy!"

Cadence turned and looked up at the large demon. He twirled Ethereal in his hand above his head, behind his back and stopped it abruptly in front of his face. He smirked, then jumped in the air and swiped the blade from left to right across Egran's throat, the deep cut separating the skin as blood sprayed and poured over the demon's neck. The demon dropped his sword and clasped both hands to his throat to try and stop the bleeding, but it kept coming; he felt dizzy and dropped on his face.

"Hell is going to make room for you. Take whatever is of value to you." Cadence twirled Ethereal in his hand one more time and held it up to get a good look at it.

"Yep! This will do."

Present Day

Cadence let slide from his jacket sleeve a sixteen-inch-blade mini-sword he called "Ethereal", meaning "heavenly light" in his hand, like a pure breeze when he swung the sword for a kill. He flipped the mini-sword around his right hand, then spun and grabbed a demon next to him and ran the blade under its chin and out the top of its head. Blood ran over Cadence's hand as a piece of skull, hair, and brains fell and slapped the concrete floor. Cadence turned, swung his sword, and sliced through the second demon's neck, separating the head from the body. It hit the wall with a hollow thud and fell to the floor. The last demon ran straight at Cadence; he spun Ethereal in his hand and ran it through the demon's right eye and out the back of the skull. When Cadence pulled the sword free, blood sprayed the wall as he flung the eyeball off the blade; it smacked the wall across from him. Jenny stared at her uncle, her mouth open. She couldn't believe her uncle could do that.

"Jenny, grab my hand — now!"

Her hand reached out, grabbing his. A stream of light from all fingers crackled and sizzled. Within seconds a black hole pulled Jenny toward the light on the other side, until she hit the ground. All wet and slimy, she smelled god-awful, like she was wearing a dress of smelly rotting meat that had been sitting in the sun for weeks. On her knees, she panted heavily, choking and gagging.

"Jenny!" someone yelled out. She looked up; it was Anne.

"A friendly face," Jenny said, with tears falling from her eyes. "Thank god, a friendly face."

Anne laughed. "So — Cade pulled you through? Shit, I didn't think he could pull it off. He was right."

"Uncle Cade!" Jenny yelled. "He told me to wait." She ran over to him and grabbed his body in her arms.

"Jenny — stop!" Anne said. "He's gone. I shot him in the head. No one can survive that. All that matters is you're safe. That's what he wanted."

Jenny bent over her uncle, crying. "No, not you, too — I have no one else. I can't handle this shit." She pounded his chest. "I have no one else, dammit!"

Anne grabbed her shoulder. "Sweetie, come on."

"Hey, you smell, and I mean god-awful!"

Jenny and Anne both looked down at Cadence. His eyes were wide, with a crooked smile forming on his mouth. A tear fell from Jenny's cheek down onto Cadence's face. With a smile, she said, "You are the bestest, uncle!"

"Don't you know it," Cadence said while smiling. Anne stood up, staring down at Cadence. None of this made sense to her. Stuff like this didn't happen; a bullet went through his brain, and he is still alive like nothing ever happened. She thought of her mother and anger set in.

Chapter 11
Meadow and Sam

Year 1798

Screams filled the bedroom. "Oh, God! Please — it hurts."

"My love," Sam said. "Calm down; this is your third child. This one should be nice and easy for you."

"Miss Leah, one last push, please," the doctor said. "You can do this — now push." She screamed louder as she gripped the wooden posts on the bed behind her. "Yes, that's it — push."

"Ahh, I'm… pushing, dammit!"

The baby pushed out and slid into the doctor's hands with a wet squishy sound, followed by the umbilical cord and slimy liquid. The placenta would follow moments later.

"It's a girl!" the doctor cheerfully said, sweat streaming down his face from exhaustion as the baby screamed to life.

"Great! I have another girl — another girl." Sam's body slumped with heavy disappointment. Every time he hoped for a boy to carry on his name, and this time he got his third girl.

"I want to name her Meadow," Leah said with tired lines on her face.

Sam looked at her with a slight snort. "OK, Meadow it is."

***

Present Day

"Sam, it worked. You were right," Cadence said with a smile on his face, walking into the store with Jenny and Anne following close behind. "This is my niece, Jenny; Jenny, this is Sam."

"So, you're Christopher's daughter," Sam said, with a smile pasted on his face.

"I am," Jenny said.

"It's a pleasure to meet you." Sam gave a slight bow and smiled like he had just met royalty.

"So, uncle, are you going to share that awesome trick with us? You know, how you pulled me back through the dark and how you came back to life?" Jenny said.

"Yeah, I would also like you to explain what happened back there," Anne said, with anger set into her emotions.

Cadence stood with a crooked smile on his face. "I told you it would freak you out — oh, by the way, you shot me in the head. I mean, in the head — and you didn't even warn me."

"Could you please just stop joking around for once, dammit?" Anne became agitated. "You're right, I shot you in the head, and you're here, HERE! Standing right here. I can't handle this shit right now. I need to go home. I'm tired and beat and fucking freaked out."

***

Year 1807

"OK, Meadow, concentrate. Palm out, yes, yes — feel the lightning." The stick with the flame at the end lifted slightly. It twitched, flew, and hit the wall; black ash flew everywhere. They were standing in the center of the courtyard, surrounded by the estate. Sam had made the yard into a training facility for his girls to practice their magic; it was spacious, with wooden stands made to look like people strategically set in various locations of the yard. They had lightning burns all over them from the practice sessions they held throughout the day.

"I'm sorry, Father." Tears were welling up in Meadow's eyes. She stomped the ground, not understanding why the lightning didn't fly off her hands the way it was supposed to.

"Meds, you are only eight years old. Don't worry, you will get the hang of it eventually."

"Hahaha, you are useless," chuckled Kaliea, standing in the shadows, clapping with delight. She was

96

five years older than Meadow and had been practicing the arts of magic for years.

"Why don't you go away and leave me alone? I can't concentrate with you staring at me with delight glowing on your face at my failures." Meadow stomped the ground and folded her arms around her waist.

"Enough, girls! Kaliea, run along and leave Meadow to her training." Sam turned his head toward the estate's entrance. He heard a traveling carriage being led by a team of horses as their hooves danced across the hard dirt that led straight to the estate.

"Samuel Locke? I have waited a long time to meet you," came a soft, slurring voice from behind the small opening on the side of the carriage. The way the sun hit the transport, all Sam could see was a strip of light across the gentleman's reddish eyes; the rest of his face was hidden behind the shadows.

"I'm impressed. Now tell me, who are you and why do you want to meet me?" Sam sternly said.

The door opened and a tall, thin man walked off the transport and stood in front of Sam. He towered over him and extended a hand. His fingers were long and bony, with nails grown out into sharp points. Sam cautiously took his hand with a firm but friendly handshake.

"My name is Lotus. Do you have time for a conversation?"

Sam stepped back and extended his arm toward the estate's front door; they entered. Lotus stopped in the foyer. It was vast and empty, and echoed when they walked. Sam's father had left him the estate when he died. Sam motioned for Lotus to sit with him in the gathering room.

"So, Lotus, what would you like to talk about?" Sam curiously asked. Lotus sat across from Sam. He sat at the edge of the chair, legs together, back straight, and hands on knees.

"Sir, have you ever heard the name Tidus Brack?"

***

Year 1716

Samuel was fifteen years old. He was staring at his father, and the three men beating him within inches of his life in the cold rain of Peillon, France. They threw Sam's father down the stairs leading to the docks where his father worked.

Pivote Locke was an older man in his late fifties, early sixties. He had heavy lines on his face and calloused hands from years of hard, honest work. Pivote was a kind man who drank a little too much, as trouble seemed to find him always.

"No, stop, leave my father alone!" Sam yelled, with black veins stemming from his neck. "Father!" His fists tightened over his palms, white-knuckled. Blood trickled down over and around his fingers while a white light built around both fists.

"Let him go — please!" The white light turned into white lightning, his fists becoming tighter and tighter. He stretched out his arms, as white lightning hit all three men and threw them back into some wood crates filled with fish. The containers splintered everywhere; blood and human flesh went flying in all directions.

"Dad, you OK?" Sam ran over to his father's side.

His father proudly looked around with a slight chuckle. "So — the men ran off, my boy?" Pivote wiped off the blood that smeared his face with his right sleeve and felt proud knowing his son had taken care of the guys beating him.

"Dad — no, they're all dead. I think something is wrong with me," Sam said, shaking his head while staring down at his hands.

"No, son, nothing is wrong with you." Pivote grabbed his boy and pulled him close. "Sam, you need to hear the truth. I have waited for the right time to tell you. It has been tough for me." Pivote looked at the ground, feeling ashamed for what he was about to tell his boy.

"Sam — you are not my son."

Sam looked over at his father with confusion on his face. "What are you trying to tell me? What do you mean, I'm not your son?"

"Sam, there was a town brutally slaughtered by another tribe that passed through your village years back. They killed everyone who stepped into their path. Women and children were no exception. Only you escaped somehow; we're not sure how. You ran for days until you ended up here in our village; you were terrified. You found shelter in our stalls. When I found you, you were cold and hadn't eaten for days. I took you in, fed you, and clothed you. I did not know about your gift. When you turned the age of eight, your eyes changed. They got darker, and they changed each year slightly from then on. You never get hurt, you feel little pain, and you heal quickly. You have watched with an awareness of everything around you, and now this — the lightning and the magic. Son, you are exceptional, and one day you will show the world how special you are."

Sam stood there and stared, not knowing what to believe. Tears were streaming down his cheeks.

***

Present Day

Cadence went to the roof of the store. He sat just at the edge with a glass and a bottle of wine. His emotions took over while he talked to himself.

"Christopher, my brother, I miss you, and I could use your help right about now. The witches are here. I killed Heather, but I don't know if I'm strong enough to take on Kaliea. She is too powerful, and I can't tell what Meadow's intentions are just yet. I don't understand how you intend to find our mother with you dying and all, but you left your daughter behind — in my hands, no less. Me — of all the people you knew. You know that I'm not a responsible person, and kids, well, annoy the hell out of me. What the hell were you thinking?"

Cadence sat there until the bottle was empty. He lay back on the rooftop. It only seemed like a few minutes before he heard an echo, a long, distant sound, flow through his head and then clear.

"So, uncle, how fun is this, waking up on the rooftop again?"

Cadence opened his eyes and saw Jenny's face looking down at him.

"So, is your head still with us? A little hungover, you are, mmm?"

"Jenny, stop with the Yoda lines, will you. Go play in traffic and leave me alone."

"Hahaha, you need to apologize to Anne. She's upset and freaked out. Besides, I know you think she's pretty, and you like her."

"Jenny, please don't." Cadence slowly stood, holding any object he could find to avoid falling.

"Uncle Cade, you haven't been with anyone in a while. I can see you're doing this because of me, like you have some obligation to take care of me twenty-four seven. I don't know if you noticed, but I'm a big girl now. I know about the birds and the bees."

"All right, that's enough, Jenny." Cadence turned around, sporting a smirk. "Did Tom tell you about the girl before my accide—?"

Jenny cut him off before he could finish his sentence. "Oh god, please — that girl doesn't count," Jenny said. "She was just a one-night stand. I'm talking about being with someone you know for more than a night. It's called a relationship."

"OK, OK, I'll go see her and apologize. Jeez!"

Jenny smiled and gave her uncle a giant hug.

"Thank you."

***

Anne walked out of her apartment to find Cadence sitting on the stoop with two cups of morning coffee and wearing a giddy smile.

"I enjoy a beautiful morning like this one. How about you? Hey, have you had breakfast yet?"

"I want you to stay away from me, Cadence Mage," Anne retorted.

"Oh, come on, Lieutenant. We're kind of like a couple now, aren't we?"

"Stop, no more joking around; it's upsetting me," Anne said. "I don't like what's going on here, just… let me go back to my simple boring life, please. I like it that way." Anne walked past Cadence and then stopped. She turned to look at him. "You know, everything from your brother to your buried friend and all your damn childhood girlfriends, witches — whatever the hell they are — except Jenny, I like her. Oh, and me? You ask me to kill you. Who does that?" Anne just stood there, staring at the ground, shaking her head.

"Yeah, and you shot me in the head. The one place I asked you not to."

"Stop! That's what I mean," Anne yelled.

Cadence put his hands up as if to indicate surrender. "OK, OK, I'm sorry. Let's talk about what you did."

"No! Go away!" Anne barked.

"Look, I've been doing this for over two hundred years, and I know what you are going through. So please, I am sorry for that, but we need each other's help. There is one skull left on that dagger, and I don't want to find out what happens when innocent blood reaches it."

There was a heavy sigh and silence for a few moments.

"All right!" Anne said. "Why did I have to run into you and your band of misfits?"

"Look, I get it, I understand, but I am the only one that knows what's going on with these murders. Now that I have my niece back, it will be easier for me to concentrate and get us through this."

"You know, you are such—" Just when the next words would be "an asshole", Anne's phone rang.

"Lieutenant Anne Black here; uh-huh, sure, all right, I'm on my way."

"Where are we going?"

Anne's jaw tightened with a straight thin line formed on her lips. "You're insane and have no grasp on reality whatsoever."

"Yes, I do!"

"No — you don't."

"Yes, I do! So, where are we going?"

Chapter 12
The Reunion

"So, Sam, what does it feel like?" Tom asked, feeling a little odd at not knowing how to speak to a five-hundred-year-old person.

"Does what feel like?" Sam looked around the room, taking it all in.

"You know — being here, in this century, seeing all the new inventions like planes, cars, oh, and television; weird, huh?"

A small, bright light started in the far corner of the room. It was baseball-sized, then softball-sized, then basketball-sized. Bits of electricity crackled from around the sphere and then there was a loud crack. Thousands of small talons formed and snapped everywhere, forming slowly with little slimy, slapping wet sounds. A figure crouched in the corner, and slowly the head rose.

"Hello, father!"

***

Cadence fell to one knee with a playful expression on his face.

"Wait — Anne, please, I'm sorry. I'm feeling terrible about this. Can you please forgive me?"

"Shut up! Just shut up!" Anne yelled.

Cadence bounced back to his feet. "So, are you going to tell me where you're off to?"

"There was another girl found downtown Fremont."

"See, I told you that you would need me."

"Can we just get going, please?"

***

"Kaliea!" Sam said with a delightful glow on his face.

"Yes, father, it's me," the phlegmy voice said. Sam stared at Kaliea, soaking in her appearance. She appeared grotesque and slimy. What had happened to his beautiful daughter?

"My *god*, daughter, what have you done with yourself?"

"Do you like it, father? I made myself beautiful." Kaliea was smiling, clapping with short, happy claps.

"Hello, Samuel." A wet slapping sound was hitting the top of the wood floor. A string of bile fell from blue-gray lips and the smell was unbearable. In the corner, shadows danced. Out stepped a tall, smelly, dark figure, hunched over. Sam turned his head to look in that direction.

106

"Where have you been, my friend? It's good to see you," the croaking voice said with a smile showing sharp rotting teeth.

***

"Cadence, please don't touch the dagger this time."

"Sorry, Anne, but—" Cadence smirked with embarrassment like a little kid. He raised his arm from behind his back; he held the dagger in his hand. Anne looked pissed at him. He gulped as his Adam's apple moved down his neck and then back into place. Three uniformed officers stared at Cadence, all chuckling at the awkward scene between him and Anne.

"There's good news, and there's bad news," Cadence said.

"Let's have the good news first," Anne said, shaking her head.

"Well, my fingerprints will not be an issue."

Anne let out a loud, heavy sigh.

"Bad news?"

"My assumption is, this is not the dagger," Cadence said.

"That's not the dagger? And how do you know this?"

"This is not The Eyes for the Souls."

Anne lost her patience. "How do you know? It looks like the dagger we've been following." Anne looked over at the other officers, annoyed and shaking her head.

"Well, there isn't any blood running from the third line to the last skull, for one."

"Great! Now we have a copycat?"

"Or — this is a diversion, to send us off-track and away from the store." Cadence thought for a moment. "Shit, we need to get to the store," he yelled. "Now!" He took off, sprinting toward the store.

***

With a big hug, Sam pulled back with a smile.

"I have missed you, my old friend."

"Same here, my brother," Lotus smiled.

"Thank you for looking after my daughters while I have been away all these years. It means a lot to me."

"Samuel, there is a problem," said Lotus, his voice sounding grossly nervous. "It's Heather."

"What about Heather? Where is she?" Sam asked with a concerned look on his face.

"She is no longer with us. It's Cadence, he… killed her."

A slight flicker came from Sam's fingertips. White lightning crackled, and his hands formed a tightened ball. His top lip curled up, exposing the gums and teeth.

"No! How did this happen? Tell me now!"

"She attacked him, trying to retrieve the dagger. Cadence, well, he finished the fight."

Sam slammed the top of Cadence's desk with both his fists.

"Dammit, he killed my daughter; does he know anything of our plans as well?"

"No, he does not know," Lotus said.

"Good, as soon as our plan pulls into shape, no one goes near Cadence, understand? I am going to kill him myself."

Tom just stood there. He couldn't move, not believing what he was seeing or hearing. He stepped back, but his hand knocked over a small candle on the desk he was standing next to, as he drew attention to himself.

"Ah! Who is this that accompanies us in the room?" Lotus asked, with more bile falling from his lips, staring at Tom.

"I'm… my name… is Tom," Tom said nervously.

"Well, hi, Tom," said Lotus. He appeared amused by Tom looking so nervous.

"Where is Cadence, and when will he be back, or has he abandoned you to let you die alone?"

"I don't know; he's out. Sam, why would you do this to him? He loves you. All he talks about is you. He calls you his father."

"Hahaha!" Kaliea laughed at what Tom said. "His father! Cadence and his pathetic brother are idiots. They don't even know who their father is."

"Kaliea! Watch your tongue," yelled Sam. Kaliea snapped her head to avoid her father's angry face. She cringed and backed into the dark. "He loves me by freezing me inside a wall for over a hundred years and then killing my daughter? Is that *real* love, Tom?"

"Your daughter killed an innocent girl, and she did this to my face; she was evil, Sam."

"Well, Tom, it was nice to have met you, but you talk too much," Lotus's voice croaked.

His hand shot out, palm side down, index finger extended slightly forward. A quick thin white lightning bolt shot from Lotus's finger and struck Tom in the chest. Tom flew back through the air and hit the wall. His breath escaped hard from his lungs. He breathed in, eyes terrified, with blood oozing out from his chest. The blood was coming from a small hole through the front and clean out the back. Blood filled Tom's mouth and dripped from his lips down his chin. His last words were, *"Oh, Cade."*

***

Cadence fell against the wall to catch his breath. His eyes flickered of light, going to dark inside his pupils.

"Cade, you OK? Talk to me," Anne said. She was right behind him with concern showing on her face.

"Something's wrong!" Cadence took off, running again in the store's direction, pushing people out of the way.

"Cade! Wait!"

Cadence ignored her and kept running. When he reached the store, as he cautiously approached the entrance, he saw the front door was ajar. It was dark and quiet inside. Cadence walked slowly as he entered the store, passing the cash register. He reached behind a bench where he kept a sawed-off shotgun just under the counter on a small, narrow shelf. Slowly and silently, while holding the gun, Cadence walked through the store, making his way back toward the office. When he reached the office entrance, Cadence crouched and cased the room, ready for any danger that might come his way. Then he saw Tom lying there on the floor, blood everywhere.

Cadence stood in disbelief and ran over to him. He fell to the floor next to him. He dropped the shotgun, grabbing Tom in his arms.

"Oh, man, Tom — what did you do now?" Cadence was shaking, holding back tears. Anne came running into the room, gun drawn, and panting.

"Cade, what's going on?" She glanced over and saw Cadence holding Tom in his arms, rocking back and forth.

"Oh no, Cadence," Anne said, "oh no."

He stared up at her, tears falling down his face.

"He was my friend."

***

Cadence sat slumped in a chair behind his desk. The LVPD had sent Tom's corpse to the morgue and were wrapping things up when Jenny walked in.

"Uncle Cade? What's happened?" She seemed scared; her eyes wide as she approached him. Cadence reached out and grabbed her arm and pulled her close, hugged her, and cried. Jenny turned her head and glanced over at Anne. She was looking down at the floor, not making eye contact with her.

"I'll be in the next room," Anne said as she walked out of the room.

Cadence backed away from Jenny, still holding her hand.

"It's Uncle Tommy," Cadence said.

Jenny's voice had a slight tremble when she spoke.

"What… happened to Tom?" Tears welled up in her eyes.

"Well," Cadence spoke softly, "he a… he is… he died earlier tonight."

"What? No, how can you say that!" Jenny barked. "No, he isn't. I just saw him. He is alive. Stop lying!"

Cadence grabbed her, pulled her close, and tightly hugged her again. He moved her to his lap. She crawled up in a fetal potion on her uncle and buried her face into his chest, crying uncontrollably.

Anne watched from the doorway. She found that her face was wet from tears; she turned and walked away and left them alone. She had seen this scene once too often.

Anne whispered to herself, "*Oh, Cade, we have a lot to talk about.*"

***

The next morning, Cadence was sitting behind his desk, trying to make sense of all this madness. "*Why is all this happening?*" he whispered. Footsteps softly stopped in front of him.

"Hello, Anne," Cadence said without looking up.

"It's time for us to talk — and I mean talk about everything that's going on."

"What do you want to know?"

"OK, first — who or what the hell are you?"

"What? I already told you who and what I am." Cadence was annoyed at the questions she was asking.

"No, you haven't told me the complete story." Anne's lips were tight in a straight line. "I want to know everything now!"

"OK, OK." Cadence put his hands up to suggest he surrendered.

"You know," Anne said, "there is a lot more going on with you than just dying and coming back to life."

"Yeah, you're right, there is; initially, I didn't understand."

"What do you mean, initially?"

"When I was younger, demons came to me in my sleep. I would see them kill, rape, and torture innocent humans. When I turned twenty years of age, I started with the worst demons and worked my way down, killing them one by one. I have done this for centuries. They call me the Demon Hunter. Now — it has stopped; I don't see the demons any more. It's quiet. I know something's wrong; something is coming. I can feel it. The demons have backed off."

"So, you think this is all connected somehow?"

"I'm not too sure, but after my brother died, I developed these unknown powers. Little by little, my hands would cramp up. I would feel this darkness spread over me when something was about to happen. The first time was at the bar when Heather walked in. I'm not sure how my body built that lightning sensation around me, or how I could grab her from across the room and do the things I did. With this — I am clueless, just as much as you are. I don't know. Maybe all this will make sense, eventually. I've had only minimal powers, minor things here and there. That's why I had to master the sword and revolver; that's what I mainly used to take down the demons. You know, my lightning helped." Cadence slammed his fist down hard on his desk in frustration.

"So, that's why you have all those swords surrounding you?"

"Yes, I have a gun collection that's just as impressive."

"OK, let's say I believe you."

"Do you?" Cadence interrupted.

"Yeah, I do, smart ass — so what's our next move here? Cade, I *am* sorry about Tom. I liked him. Jenny seems like she's taking it hard. Is she OK?" Anne's face was overtaken with sympathy.

"Yeah, she's a tough girl. She'll be all right. Now, we have one problem."

"What's that?"

"Well, the dagger. What kind of blood are they targeting? Who are they targeting? When and where will be their next move, and why did they try to throw us off the track with a fake dagger? But I know one thing." Anne tilted her head, looking at Cadence as he spoke. "We cannot let the blood reach that last skull."

***

Later that night, Cadence was tossing and turning while trying to sleep. Sweat glistened over his body and puddled beneath him. A large demon stood in front of him. Cadence stared up at him; and with a heavy sigh Cadence spoke.

"Let me guess, you are here to kill me."

"You certainly don't look like a demon hunter, boy," the large demon croaked.

"Yeah, well sorry to disappoint." Ethereal slid silently down his forearm until he firmly held the blade in his hand. The demon raised his enormous axe high above his head and let it fall. Cadence smiled and held up Ethereal. As the axe clashed with the blade, Cadence on one knee spun around to the backside of the large demon and sliced through his left Achilles, then swiftly through his right. The demon fell to his knees and cried out in pain. Suddenly, there was a loud screech! "Eeeech! Cade!"

Both Cadence and the large demon turned their heads. Cadence sent his lips close to the demon's ear.

"Wait for me right here, demon; I will be back to finish you off and send you back to hell."

"Nooo!" the demon cried out.

Cadence's eyes flew open as he sat straight up in his bed. He saw a body outlined in the shadows. The head turned sideways, and the mouth shot upward from the top lip, brown drool falling from the bottom lip. The skin drooped down, hanging from the tilted side of the cheek.

"*Kaliea is coming for you,*" the creature said.

"What?" Cadence said, still a little groggy from being scared straight out of his sleep from the scream. "What the hell, who are you?" Cadence barked back into the darkness.

The thing's head straightened out. The top lip went down to smooth, thin, beautifully lined lips. Its skin slowly smoothed out, and beautiful strands of strawberry blonde hair grew out.

"Meadow?" Cadence whispered. "Is that you?"

"Yes, Cade, it's me," Meadow said with the most beautiful soft whisper that flowed through his ears. Cadence closed his eyes to remember how he used to love when she whispered into his ear after a long night of passionate lovemaking. She reached forward and set her lips on Cadence's lips with a long, slow, passionate kiss. Cadence sounded confused when he spoke.

"Wha— what did you say earlier?"

"I said Kaliea is coming for you — quick, she is here."

There was a loud crash! Like an explosion.

"*Hello, Cady!*" he heard as Kaliea melted into view.

Chapter 13
Kaliea Locke

Cadence flew off the bed, twisted to his right, and grabbed the revolver next to him on the nightstand. He turned, cocked back the hammer, and pointed.

"Fuck you, Kaliea!"

With a slight squeeze of the trigger, a single bullet spiraled through the barrel. Smoke surrounded the opening of the barrel as the bullet exited toward Kaliea. Kaliea moved to her left and shot out her hand. A wave hit the bullet and sent it flying a safe distance into the plastered wall, out of harm's way.

"Oh, Cady, please," Kaliea said with a wry smile.

Cadence gagged and smelled something so rank, with a sickly rotting smell. Cadence slipped a little, looked down, and saw a puddle of dark slime pooling around his feet. There was a slight pain. The skin from the front of Cadence's chest stretched out suddenly with a sickening sound — snap! The blade of a sword glistened through his chest, blood dripping off the thin sharp edge.

"Goddammit!" Cadence said, wincing in pain. "Don't you idiots know I can't die?" As he turned around, a white bolt of lightning hit him and knocked him clear across the room. Cadence flew into the bookshelf. He raised his head with blood pooling from his mouth, laughing. Standing across the room, with long black slimy hair and shadows hiding his face, stood Lotus.

"I give up, who are you?" Cadence asked, still laughing.

"You don't remember me?" Lotus asked, annoyed that Cadence didn't remember their moment together.

"Why, darling," Kaliea said, "meet Lotus."

Anger shot through Cadence. His veins darkened through his neck, arms, and all the rest of his body. He slightly elevated off the ground. His eyes rolled back in his head to expose a black ink-like texture moving through the white of his eyes. Kaliea backed away with fear on her face.

"Cade? What the hell is going on?" she asked, backing up. Cadence elevated higher.

"Lotus, you dare come here and try to kill me in my own home!" Cadence growled while glaring at Lotus.

Lotus, with a smile, built up energy through his body with outstretched arms, ready to send an attack on Cadence.

"I think you will die just as easily as your sniveling weak friend did. What was his name? Oh, yes, Tom, I believe it was."

Right before Lotus lifted his arms, Cadence flew across the room at Lotus, screaming. Behind him, the light followed in a stream. He stopped in front of Lotus.

He reached out and grabbed hold of Lotus's head. Slowly he twisted back and forth while lifting upward. Lotus screamed. Cadence pulled with ease, as tendons and skin stretched and ripped apart. Blood flowed from his neck, mouth, and nose.

"You son of a bitch!" Cadence's upper lip curled up, exposing clenched teeth. "You killed my friend Tom!" All the while he continued to pull and twist, until there was a wet, sloppy, ripping, popping sound. Lotus's head finally separated from his body. Kaliea screamed and disappeared from the room.

Lotus's body fell to the floor, splashing in his dark-brown smelly slime. Cadence kicked the body across the room with ease, dropping the head on the floor. He lifted his leg, slammed his foot hard on top of the head, and caved in the face with a crunching sound. A gooey slime oozed from the skull all around Cadence's feet as he stared down, admiring what he had just done.

"Asshole!" Cadence fell to the floor. Slowly, the black veins disappeared as he fell back into himself — but not before Jenny was standing in the doorway crying, her mouth open wide.

"*Uncle Cade?*" she whispered. "Wha— what's happening to you? How did you do that? Shit, that was gross."

Cadence looked at Jenny and then around the room, noticing that Kaliea was not present; he felt his anger grow as he yelled out, "Kaliea!" He took off, running toward the window. Without a care, he flew and crashed through it. Glass shattered everywhere. Jenny threw her arms in front of her face as glass shards stabbed at her.

"YOU BITCH!" Cadence flew after Kaliea.

"Go to hell, stay away from me!" she yelled as she whipped through the dark alleys, Cadence right behind her. Kaliea slammed to the right, hit the corner wall, and stucco went flying in pieces.

Cadence flew right in line behind her. He reached back and released a lightning bolt from his hand and hit Kaliea; she went tumbling. She scrambled to her feet, running to the left and around the corner so fast she was just a blur.

"YOU BITCH!" Cadence screamed again. He reached her, he grabbed her by the hair, and slammed her to the ground and onto her back. When she hit, it was like a wrecking ball as she smashed the ground hard; asphalt and dirt went flying up.

"Get away from me. What the fuck are you? My god," Kaliea screamed back in fear. "How… are you able to do this? Where is this strength coming from?"

Cadence smashed his foot to the ground with a thunderous shake. It reached three or four feet in front of him. It knocked Kaliea off her feet again; his foot slammed, again and again, Kaliea screamed.

"You killed Tom, and now it's your turn, bitch!"

"That wasn't me; Lotus killed your friend," she screamed with fear.

Cadence fell to his knees, with shadows and wind surrounding him, his arms outstretched. The darkness spread through him. He shot both hands close together, as a ball of darkness, with a slight stream of gray, shot forward. Kaliea screamed. Just before the darkness spread over her, Sam appeared. He stared at Cadence. He smiled and grabbed Kaliea. They both disappeared as the black ball hit the wall and ash puffed everywhere. Cadence fell to the ground with anger still on his face, baring his teeth and breathing heavily.

"Goddammit!" Cadence slowly got up and walked back to his place. He walked in and saw nobody was there, not even Lotus's body and the separated caved-in head; even the window was restored. He didn't care; he felt drained of his energy. He walked over to the bed, stripped off his clothes, and plopped down and fell into a deep sleep.

***

"Cade! Come on, wake the hell up!" yelled Anne, shaking Cadence from his shoulder. With a little sleepiness in his eyes, he sat up, pulled the covers back, and stood.

"Whoa, whoa, more than I can handle there, Tex — come on, Jesus, clothes?"

Anne looked away and then glanced over quickly to look once more. She couldn't believe how beautiful Cadence's body looked. With a wry smile, she turned away again.

"Oh, sorry," Cadence yelped as he pulled the blanket back around himself. "Why are you here?"

"Well, I don't know. Jenny called me, hysterically crying to come and help you. She said that Kaliea and the tall smelly man were attacking you."

"Shit, my head; why are you yelling?" Cadence shook his head.

Anne let out a long sigh. "OK, how much did you have to drink last night?"

"Not enough, I'm just feeling drained — man, can you just leave me alone?"

"I would, but Jenny seemed very upset when she called me."

"Hey, Uncle Cade, you OK?" Jenny was standing in the doorway of the bedroom, looking upset.

"Why? What did you see last night? What did I do?" Cadence looked confused.

"Uncle — you were floating in the air. All your veins and eyes turned black; oh, and you ripped the head off that gross tall smelly man Lotus. Then you flew out the window like Superman. So, why am I asking if you're OK? Something is wrong with you; and what happened to the body — and the window?" Jenny said, pointing at the window where Cadence had played Superman. Cadence thought to himself, how did Jenny see him while he was battling in the dreamworld?

"Yeah, what she said!" Anne barked, thumbing over in Jenny's direction.

Cadence looked over at Anne. "Well, what do you think of me now? Impressive, huh?"

"You're a dick. You know that, right?"

"Yeah, yeah, I know. Jen, honey, I'm not sure why all that happened with the body or anything else. All I know is I am immortal. But things are happening I'm not able to explain. When your dad passed, he told me unexplained things would start to happen. I didn't know what he meant by that, but I am slowly understanding. I am developing new powers, ones I have to say I do not want because they are scaring the hell out of me, and they hurt. We still need to figure out the dagger situation — oh, and do me a favor, can you leave the room so I can put my pants on, will ya?" Cadence looked over at Anne. "I don't need you staring at me like that; it makes me uncomfortable," Cadence said as he let out a wet-sounding snort.

"How about take a shower first," Anne and Jenny said as they left the room, closing the door behind them. Cadence dropped the blanket and started toward the shower, smelling his armpit. "I don't smell that bad," he said to himself.

Anne yelled through the closed door, "Yeah, you do."

Cadence laughed and stepped under the water.

"Hey, Cade, where has Sam been?" Anne asked.

"Sam, he is no longer on our side. He is part of the dagger murders, along with his daughter Kaliea." He took in a deep breath and slowly let it out. "Meadow warned me last night. Shit, I didn't see this coming."

"Wait! Meadow, the younger witch, warned you?"

"Yes, *that* witch," Cadence snapped sarcastically while vigorously scrubbing his head with shampoo. "Jeez, Anne, what's wrong with you? Have you not been listening?"

"Nothing is wrong. It's just — oh, God! Sorry, I forgot you two were an item, back in the day."

"No — yes! But it was a long time ago." Cadence was embarrassed by the statement.

"Oh — how long?" Anne asked with the back of her head leaning against the bedroom door.

"I don't know, close to a hundred years, I guess, give or take a little."

Emotions settled inside Anne.

"Oh — OK, I guess that's why she warned you of her sisters, then." Anne felt jealous and lonely as her feelings stirred for Cadence; she blushed.

"I don't know why she warned me. That's what I can't figure out. I haven't seen or spoken to her for a long time."

Anne's phone rang.

"This is Lieutenant Anne Black; uh-huh, sure, be there as soon as I can."

"Hey, Anne, want to wash my back for me? Hello? Anne — you there — hello?"

***

"So, you tried to kill Cadence without running it by me?" Sam asked with annoyance in his voice.

"Yes, I did, Father. He's — I don't know. He's stronger. I felt it from my first encounter with him a few weeks ago."

"We need the dagger complete if we are to penetrate the dark side of his soul, to unlock all of his powers so we can defeat him!" Sam slammed his fist down hard on the table.

"Don't you think I know this, Father?"

"Watch your goddamn tongue, daughter, if you don't want me to impale it against that wall!" Sam yelled louder.

"The first fail was with his mother all those years ago, and that was very unfortunate. We will make sure we do not fail again. Tidus will not tolerate it — or there will be severe consequences for all of us if we do."

***

Cadence got out of the shower, dried off, and wiped the steam and condensation from the mirror. He sighed, staring back at himself. *"Shit, what is going on?"* he whispered. He walked over to the bed and slid into his pants. Cadence looked around the bedroom. It had a queen-size bed, a nightstand, and a dust-filled bookcase. He thought to himself, *"Man, I need to get more furniture."* He pulled a T-shirt over his head and let it fall over his body. Cadence walked back into the bathroom and looked at himself in the mirror and sighed.

The mirror shattered out toward Cadence. In the middle of all the shards were two hands, followed by the face of Kaliea. She was screaming! Cadence moved to his left, rolled over the bed, and slammed into the wall. He hit the dresser drawer with the side of his fist; he reached in and grabbed two revolvers. He raised his arms straight at Kaliea and fired both guns. She contorted her body in all directions so that not one bullet hit her. Cadence looked at his guns and then back at her. "Shit — I missed."

Her hands smacked together as she threw her arms toward Cadence. A ball of fire flew directly at him; his eyes widened as he ducked just before being hit with the fireball.

Cadence jumped to his feet. He lifted the bed with one hand and flipped it at Kaliea. It hit her as she slammed against the wall. Kaliea's anger lifted her strength, as she flew across the room. Cadence stood up, lightning zapping around his body as Kaliea hit him. She wrapped her arms and legs around him. A big white ball of lightning wrapped around her and sent her flying across the room. Cadence stood there, arms out and fists formed.

"Where is Meadow?" Cadence screamed. "What have you done with her?"

Kaliea lay there laughing, blood dripping from her mouth. "I haven't seen or heard from Meadow for decades. Why are you saying her name after what you did to her?"

"You mean after what you did to her," Cadence said.

"Hahaha, you were not right for her, Cady, but you couldn't see that, could you? She loved you. She worshipped you, and you, what — walked away from her?"

"This has nothing to do with the situation at hand," Cadence said.

"No, it doesn't," came a voice from the corner of the room. His face was barely lit from the low lighting.

"Sam — you never cease to amaze me. You're my friend, and then you become my enemy."

Kaliea slowly got to her feet, feeling secure now her daddy was there, and she wiped the blood from her mouth.

"So, Sam, what's with the dagger?"

"Oh, Cade." Sam stepped into the light. "If you only knew."

"If I only knew what?"

"Cadence, you are hindering all that we have set into motion since you were a boy."

"Yeah, well — you know that's me, always getting in the way of a good diabolical scheme." Cadence rolled his eyes. "So, Sammy, why the blood? What's so special about the blood?"

"NO MORE TALKING!" yelled Sam.

Sam's face contorted, his teeth ripped into his gums; they were replaced by sharp yellow-greenish ones. His skin turned milky white and became loose on his bones. His voice grew harsh.

"Ssstay… Aaawayy…! Do not…"

"Yeah, yeah, whatever," Cadence interrupted, not the least bit bothered by Sam's appearance.

Sam picked Cadence up off the floor and slammed him down to the ground. Cadence hit the floor hard. Sam's top lip curled back, baring his greenish teeth. Standing over Cadence's body, all contorted, drool slid from his bottom lip. A long drop of slimy spit landed on Cadence's cheek and made its way to the corner of his mouth. Cadence gagged and coughed. Sam just stood there over Cadence.

"We will never speak of this again!" Sam roared.

Cadence rolled over and threw up a lot of yellow bile. Kaliea made a face of disgust and turned away. Sam backed up into the shadows until they swallowed his milky white skin. All the while, he was laughing.

Kaliea looked over with a nervous expression, and then she vanished.

Cadence stood, feeling beaten up and talking to himself. "*Man, Kaliea keeps beating the shit out of me. Goddammit, what's the blood for that's feeding that dagger?*" He picked up the phone and called Anne.

"This is Lieutenant Anne Black."

"Hey!" Cadence said on the other end of the phone. "Can you meet me at the store?"

"I'm a little busy at the moment."

"Yeah, I know, but this is important."

"Important, huh? Important, how?"

"Yeah, important — like, dagger important."

A heavy sigh came from Anne on the other end. "Oh, all right, I'll be there in twenty minutes."

"Hey, can you grab me a bottle of wine on the way? I'm out—"

"Oh, shut up!" Anne said, shaking her head. All she heard was a little chuckle and a thank you right before she hung up the phone.

***

"Well, I'm here. I hope pulling me away from that homicide was worth it —oh, and here is your bottle." Anne placed the wine on the table and looked at Cadence. "Holy shit! Your face. What happened to you? Are you all right?"

"Yeah, I'm good. Kaliea and Sam paid me a brief visit earlier after you left."

"Jesus, Cade, she's relentless."

"I'm fine, no need to get all googly over me."

"Whatever." Anne shook her head. "So, what's this all about?"

Cadence opened cabinet drawers and looked on bookshelves, trying to find a corkscrew. "Ah, here it is.

Well, Anne, we need to figure out this whole thing, and why they are using the blood to activate the dagger." The cork from the wine bottle made a POP! It startled Anne; Cadence smiled.

Chapter 14
Embracing Death

Two weeks passed, and Cadence had not heard from Kaliea or Sam, and he didn't have any new leads on the dagger. Jenny was still upset over Tom's death. She sat silently behind the counter of the store next to the cash register; only when a customer came in to make a purchase, did she talk.

Why can't I figure this out? Cadence was playing it out in his head while sitting at his desk in the back office. *Why are they using the three-headed dagger? What will the blood do when it reaches the last head? More important, why are they collecting the blood? Is it special blood or just any blood? Damn, too many questions and no answers.*

Cadence rested his head in his hands. He sighed, stood up, and walked around the room, thinking of Tom, thinking of Kaliea and Sam, trying to make sense of it all. Where the hell had Anne been?

A tear slid down his right cheek as he felt his anger set in. He tightened his hands into fists and then opened them again. He spread his fingers, as white-blue lightning danced through and licked at his fingers as he played with it. *Shit, Tom.*

***

Anne finished a relaxing hot bath. Then she toweled off and wrapped the soft towel around her beautiful curves. She walked into the bedroom, then sat down on the end of the bed. The nightly news was on the TV, but she didn't care. All she kept thinking about was what she had witnessed over the last month. She shot Cadence in the head, and he came back to life. That's shit you see in the movies or read about in fantasy books.

She laid down on the bed with a soft pillow under her head. She fell unconscious quickly. It seemed like only moments later that Anne's body shot straight up when she heard a loud bang from the living room. She sat up, dazed from a deep sleep that the sound had abruptly woken her from. It was dark; the only stream of light came from the ending broadcast on the TV across from the bedroom.

Anne reached over to the nightstand where her Glock was lying loosely in the leather holster. She slowly stood, trying not to make a noise, then walked silently toward the hallway that led to the living room. Anne raised her Glock in both hands, eyeing down the gun's sight, ready for anything that jumped out at her from where it might be hiding in the dark.

She crept into the room; her eyes quickly adjusted to the dark. Sweat rolled off her forehead and down the bridge of her nose. Fear engulfed her to the point that she was breathing short, quick breaths. Anne moved around and felt the wall for the light switch. She found it and clicked it on and raised the gun fast and ready.

The lamp on the corner table was no longer there, but was lying on the floor, smashed into pieces. A furry white cat peeked out from behind the table leg.

"Mr Doyle!" Anne whispered out loud. "Did you do that, Mr Doyle?"

She had named the cat after a character from her favorite movie, *The French Connection*.

Anne let out a sigh and stood up straight. *Fuck, this shit is too much.* She went back to the bedroom and sat on the floor. She leaned against the bed, still holding her Glock, cocked and ready, for the rest of the night until daylight streamed through the blinds.

***

Early morning, Jenny turned the key in the lock that led to the store, opened the door, turned the sign around to "Yes, We're Open" and walked in. She opened the store every morning and got it ready for customers. Same old routine every day, she thought to herself. The phone rang from the back office. Her uncle was already back there; he picked up the phone.

"Hello?" she heard her uncle say. He must have slept there last night. "Anne, where have you been? Should I be concerned?" he continued.

Jenny walked into the office and leaned against the doorjamb, listening.

"OK, I'll come over; be there soon, all right? I'm leaving now."

"So that was Anne? How is she? Where has she been?" Jenny had a thousand questions for Cadence to answer.

"She sounds fine," Cadence said while putting on his jacket. "Listen, she asked me to come over. She wants to talk; it won't take long. Can you mind the store without me for a while? Will you be good while I'm out? Anything you need that I can bring back for you?"

"Sure, I can watch the store. You know — just go. I'll be *right* here, as always."

Cadence stopped in his tracks, hearing the sarcasm in her voice. "Want to come with me? We can go to see Anne together."

Jenny thought for a moment. "No, go. I need to take care of the store and tend to the customers. Go ahead, please, just go."

***

There was a knock at the door. Anne was still sitting on the floor at the end of the bed. She hadn't moved all night. Her head snapped up at the knocking sound coming from the door.

"Hey! Anne, you in there?" A few moments passed. He heard the deadbolt to the door slide back, and the chain clanked while it was dropped. The door creaked open to a narrow crack. A beautiful blue-green eye appeared. It stared at Cadence for a moment, and then the door swung open.

"Come in and hurry," Anne said nervously, and grabbed Cadence by the arm, pulling him into the apartment. She poked her head out and swung it from left to right; she saw her neighbor down the hall. Anne sent a weak smile and a wave to the older lady, then closed the door behind her. She slammed the deadbolt and chain back into place as Cadence noticed the gun in her hand. The apartment was a mess, like she didn't care about cleaning. Anne seemed a mess herself, with knotted hair, sweatpants, and a large T-shirt.

"Anne, what's going on? You don't look so good. Everything OK?"

"I can't stop thinking about what I've done to you and what happened after." Anne put her hand affectionately on Cadence's cheek. He kept eyeing the gun in her hand; her hand was shaky, which made him nervous. "I keep hearing noises in the dark rooms. When I go to check the rooms, nothing is there. I know they can pop up wherever and when they want. It's driving me insane."

"Anne, why don't you come back to the store with me? Stay with Jenny and me for a while. You will be safe there, and I can watch over you until we figure this out."

"Yeah, yeah, sure," Anne whispered. "I'd like that."

"All right, let's do this. Oh! Please take a shower first. Trust me, you need one."

"OK! I get it, dammit. I'll take a shower. Man, you never quit, I guess that's what I like about you."

Cadence snorted as he sat on the couch and turned on the TV, waiting for Anne to complete her shower.

***

Anne and Cadence turned down a side street headed toward old Las Vegas, trying to get to the store.

"Look, Anne, I'm sorry I got you mixed up in all this. I understand you can't get a handle on what is going on here. You are not the first to freak out, seeing these strange and horrible images."

Anne walked in silence, head down, arms folded tight around herself. They both walked in silence for about ten minutes. Cadence gingerly grabbed Anne by the arm, stopped, and turned her toward him.

"You will never get used to the darkness I have exposed you to." Cadence stared into her beautiful blue-green eyes. "I don't expect you to, but we must find the three-headed dagger." Tears slid down her cheeks. Cadence smiled, reached up, and gently wiped her tears away.

"Come on, let's get to the store."

***

"Hey, Jenny!" Cadence yelled out. "Where are you? Anne is here; come on and say hi. Huh, that's weird, she could be in the back. Let's find her. She misses you, you know."

"Hey Jenny!" With a cheerful voice, he opened the door to his office and walked in.

"Hello, Cade." Sam was sitting behind Cadence's desk, feet propped up, sporting a big smile.

Cadence glanced into the darkness of the room. Jenny was sitting in a chair, crying. The room felt cold and damp, and in the shadows behind Jenny was some movement. Arms were slowly caressing Jenny's waist as the shadows spread open and Kaliea's face came into view. The light surrounded her face, exposing the sickly mess, with her eyes sunk into the top of her cheekbones.

"Hi, Cady," Kaliea said. "Now this is a party," she said in a slurring, sick-sounding voice.

"Uncle Cade?" Jenny said with a shaky voice, crying louder this time.

Cadence could see Kaliea crouched behind the chair with her arms squeezing tighter around Jenny's waist.

"I see you brought your girlfriend with you. She going to fight your battles for you, too?" Kaliea said with a sickly laugh through the bile and phlegm rolling around inside the top of her throat.

Anne reached to her side and removed her Glock and pointed it straight at Kaliea. "You know, bitch, if you're looking for a fight, I'll be happy to go a few rounds with you."

"Come on, Sam. You still pissed I froze you in that wall all those years ago?"

"Cadence, you are a bright young man. You think that is the only reason I am upset? YOU KILLED MY DAUGHTER!" Sam's feet came off the desktop as he shot forward with both hands, showing a slight crackle of lightning.

"Now I am about to kill your other daughter, Sam, if Kaliea doesn't take her hands away from Jenny." Cadence's top lip curled up. He was exposing teeth and saliva, glowering at Kaliea while avoiding eye contact with Sam. Kaliea showed a hint of fear. She didn't like the way Cadence was staring at her.

The meaty lump on the back of Cadence's neck moved, like a poached egg flipping around in boiling water.

"Cade, your neck — it's—" Anne turned away in disgust.

The lump split open and peeled back, exposing a light. This orange-red lightning slowly circled Cadence, starting at his feet as it licked its way up his body like flames on a log. Kaliea's eyes widened as she stood there watching the cocoon-like lightning mixed with flames engulfing his body.

"Well, this is something new," Jenny said with a look of astonishment. Right before the lightning touched his head, his eyes turned orange-red. Cadence's right arm shot out straight. Bolts of fire lightning shot from his hand. They hit Sam and sent him flying from the desk and slammed him into the wall, pinning him there. Sam tried to move, but the lightning was tight around his body; he wiggled back and forth, but couldn't move. Then Cadence's left arm shot toward Kaliea. The lightning grew talons and grabbed her by the neck. He lifted her off the floor and threw her across the room with such a force she went right through the wall. Wood splinters and drywall flew in all directions. Anne had to jump out of the way to prevent Kaliea's body from slamming into her.

"I SAID, GET YOUR HANDS OFF OF JENNY!" Cadence screamed.

"Now you will die!" Sam's voice contorted with a deep growl as his anger took priority over his plans. Sam lifted both his arms up high over his head and swung them down and pounded the ground. The desk, chairs, and the chair that Jenny was sitting in lifted from the floor, then slammed back down hard to the ground.

Cadence just stood there, unfazed by the boom! Anne fell hard to the ground, losing her grip on her Glock. Jenny came down as the chair snapped and splintered beneath her, setting her free.

Cadence grabbed Sam with lightning talons and slammed him back into the wall and shattered the window. Glass shards fell all around him.

"Father!" Kaliea screamed. "You mustn't kill Cade; we need him for the ritual!"

Cadence snapped his head over and stared in Kaliea's direction. He looked back over at Sam, seeing the broken glass shattered on the floor. From a distance, Cadence picked up the shards with a swift motion of his hand and threw them at Kaliea. They flew across the room and sliced into her like she was warm butter. One shard opened up her side, slicing the skin open, exposing the pink flesh and muscle just under the ribs. The second shard pierced her right eye, stopping right before stabbing into the brain behind the socket, snapping her head back. All the other shards were slicing and opening wounds around her skin on various areas of her body, causing blood to shoot out of her in all directions.

"Kaliea!" Sam yelled out. Sam flew over to Kaliea with amazing speed, black-gray smoke trailing behind him. He picked Kaliea up in his arms and shot a look back over at Cadence with blood and hate in his eyes.

"You think this is over? You better look over your shoulder for now and make sure that all the bumps in the night and the dark corners are not me!" Sam held Kaliea close. The black-gray smoke surrounded them; then they disappeared.

"Jenny, are you all right?"

"Yeah, I'm fine," Jenny stood, wiping herself off from all the dust and debris flying around the room.

"Are you good, Anne?" Cadence looked over at her.

"I am not even going to ask how the hell you did that. I will just put it in the book of Cadence — just another normal day."

Cadence chuckled, still staring at Anne. He thought to himself how beautiful and strong she was, and he enjoyed the way she looked back at him. Cadence's lips formed a smile, then went to a straight line. His eyes widened as Anne's smile went away and she cocked her head slightly to one side. She looked over at Cadence, wondering why he had that look on his face, and then she looked over at Jenny. She had the same look.

"What's wrong, guys?" Pain shot through her, starting from her back. When she looked down, she saw her skin stretch further and further as a hand popped through. It was a loud pop, and painful. Tears streamed down her face as she saw her heart still pumping in the hand — meat and blood slapping the floor, mixed with bone and cloth from her shirt.

Slowly rising from behind Anne stood Sam. The way the light hit his face set the evil he was. He put his lips close to her ear and whispered, "*This will piss Cade off. I think he likes you.*"

The last thing Anne could smell was his foul breath.

"*I love the way you smell. It's like almonds, death, and Cadence's hate for me all floating together,*" Sam whispered again, with a soft, evil laugh, his rotting breath lingering. "*Your heartbeats are slowing down. It's tickling the palm of my hand.*"

Anne breathed her last breath.

"*Anne, it's Mommy!*"

Anne extended her arms out. "*Mommy!*" Tears were falling down her face. "*Why?*"

Her mother looked at her and raised her arm, pointed, and then whispered, *"Why? Because you stopped believing!"*

Chapter 15
Meadow Locke

"Anne Black, beloved daughter of Lillian and Joseph Black, 1987–2019," Cadence read as he stared down at the headstone. Tears filled the bottom lids of his eyes as he knelt and laid flowers in front of her headstone. Cadence spoke to Anne's headstone. "I'm sorry, Anne, I should have never gotten you involved in all this mess. I never meant for this to happen." Cadence stood there, head down in silence, playing it all in his head.

"*Hello, Cady,*" a voice whispered close in his ear. "*Look what my father did.*"

Cadence turned around, and there stood Meadow. She was so beautiful standing with the sun behind her, her body outlined behind the dress she wore. It showed every curve. Cadence couldn't move; he could only stare.

***

Kaliea had just disappeared from the room.

"Goddammit, Meadow, what's wrong with that bitch sister of yours? She thinks she is your mother. She barges in here whenever she wants and starts all this shit with you. It's pissing me off," Cadence said, still lying in bed naked, with the sheets draped over his lower half.

Meadow walked back over to the bed, pulled the sheets back, and slid against Cadence's warm naked body, wrapping the linen back around their bodies. Cadence put his face in the crook of her neck and breathed in. She had a slight smell of vanilla and sex roaming around her beautiful skin and curves. Meadow ran her foot up and down Cadence's leg.

"So — are we getting all worked up? Want to go again, handsome?"

"Come on, Meds. She doesn't bother you, her coming in here and screaming at you, throwing her magic around like that?"

"She is my older sister. She's just trying to protect me, that's all. She is harmless." Meadow nibbled on his earlobe, hoping to make him a little excited.

"Stop it!" Cadence pulled playfully away from her. She touched his earlobe. "Stop it!" She put her tongue in his ear. "Stop it!" Meadow playfully laughed. "She doesn't like me — as a matter of fact, your entire family hates me, except your father. Why is that? What the hell did I ever do to them?"

"Heather is filling Kaliea's head with all these stories and lies, and it's stuck in their heads you will hurt me one day. So — will you?"

Meadow laughed and rolled on top of Cadence. Cadence grabbed her and rolled her over so he was on top; he entered her with a stern thrust.

"Oh, yeah, babe; I'm gonna hurt you all right."

***

Present Day

With a slight breeze and the hot desert sun beaming on Cadence's face, he looked up to face Meadow.

"What the hell is going on, Meds?" Cadence's annoyance was prominently showing; he realized he sounded a little upset. He grinded his teeth and softly whispered through them. "Sam killed her; he didn't have to do that. Your father only did it because he knew it would upset me, and understand this — Sam will pay with his life for what he has done."

"Cade, he wants this from you. He wants you to lose your control and come after him. Don't you see this?"

"She was innocent in all of this. Med; he didn't have to kill her, and you know that."

"Cade, listen now — no more grieving. I don't have long. My father and Kaliea could be watching us. They are not aware I am talking to you; hell, they don't even

146

know I am back. Only Heather knew, but you got to her before she told Kaliea about me.”

“Tom told me you helped him that night when Heather attacked him. Thank you.”

“Yeah, the poor guy looked defenseless in that fetal position, crying and bleeding all over the place. I felt sorry for the little guy, but I needed to get your attention, so I took a chance and exposed myself. Now listen, Cade. The Eyes for the Souls only needs one more stabbing before it is complete. When the blood reaches the last skull, Father will have the power to control the souls imprisoned by the dagger. Then they will come for *you*. I’m not sure if it will be one by one or all at once. Either way, they will come for you. They want to harness your powers.”

The breeze became a wind, and the heat turned into a chill. The clouds rolled in with a gray tint to them. Cadence stood there, staring at Meadow, his hair moving and flowing with the wind.

“Well, what the hell is he going to do with *my* powers?”

“He is coming after *you*, Cade. You need to figure out why and then be ready for him.” Meadow’s whispers blended with the wind twisting around them. “I have to go, Cady; Kaliea feels like she is close.” She sounded nervous and looked around as if looking for someone.

“Wait, I have more questions to ask you,” Cadence asked louder over the wind building up around him. He saw black-gray smoke swirl around Meadow’s body.

As she was disappearing, Cadence heard a faint whisper, *"When the time is right, I will come to you again."*

"When will that be? How will I know?"

"Soon — I love you, Cadence." Then she disappeared.

Why is Sam coming after me? *What does he want with my powers? Did she just say — she loved me?* Cadence shook off that notion, looked back at Anne's grave once more, turned, and bent down to fix the flowers that had blown over from the wind. Cadence set his hand on the headstone and whisked away the dust that had accumulated; he stood back up, still looking down at her grave, wiped away the tears streaming down his cheeks, and walked down the path toward the entrance. There was a soft, quick, and happy sickly laugh echoing in the distance, then it disappeared. Cadence stopped and looked around the cemetery, investigating the area. He shook his head, chuckled, and walked toward the entrance. When the cell phone in his pocket rang, he pulled it out and looked at it; he hit the accept button.

"Hey, Jenny, everything all right? Yeah, I'm on my way. See you soon." He hung up, put the phone back in his pocket, wiped another tear from his cheek, and headed for the store.

Chapter 16
The Third Kill

Somewhere in downtown old Las Vegas in a murky Motel 6, Room 12, on the second floor, curtains were closed tightly, not letting any light shine through.

"Kaliea, it's almost time." Sam sat over in the corner, behind the dark, with shadows dancing around him.

Kaliea groaned, rolled over, and sat up on the bed. Her wounds were still healing from the fight with Cadence. "Yes, I can feel it. My body should start that slight burning sensation any day now."

"We do this tomorrow night, no matter what, so you better burn," Sam whispered. He sighed, stood up, and walked over to the table.

"Father, do you think this will work?"

Ignoring his daughter, he stood at the table. His fingers traced over the carvings etched in the old, worn box that sat at the edge of the bed. His finger found a small pin made of human bone and he removed it from the slot. The lid popped. Dust floated out from all four corners of the box and mixed with the surrounding air. Sam flicked the top open with his forefinger in one quick upward snap. Inside, the box had a purple-black velvet lining that caressed the dagger. It had three skulls carved in human bone. Sam picked up the dagger and held it to the light. "*Soon, you will be free,*" he said to himself.

***

"Kaliea, are you feeling the burn yet?" Sam grabbed her by the arm and led her straight through a dark street on a hot and dry night. She looked around frantically, looking for the one with the blood that would fill the third and final skull on the dagger.

"Father, the pig is close; she's not far. I can feel the warmth of her body. She's in that crowd of people just ahead." Kaliea pursed her lips. "Hmm, she's close."

Sam threw Kaliea to the ground. He knelt next to her and grabbed her by the face and squeezed. "Find her now and make it soon." He was grinding his teeth, talking tightly through them at his daughter.

"Father, I said she's here," Kaliea said nervously.

The girl had dirty blonde hair and was beautiful, with a long smooth neck; a black lace choker caressed it. Her skin was a milky white color, and she had a slim body. Kaliea stared, her eyes fixated, looking straight at her. She drooled brown-green saliva that slowly trailed down her chin and formed a long spit line. It stretched until it finally broke off and slapped the pavement by her feet.

"There, Father." She pointed into the Vegas crowd. Kaliea's head tilted back. Her sunken eyes closed as she could see the outline of the beautifully shaped woman.

"Father, can I please have the pig after you slaughter her? I have plans for the body."

"All I need is her blood to complete the dagger. After that, I do not care what you do with her. You can slice her open and crawl up inside her body and fester until she rots, for all I care. Get the fucking blood — do you understand?"

"Thank you, Father. Oh, how I am looking forward to playing with her, her skin — the smell." Kaliea smiled as she pulled a small blade from her sleeve and sliced her forearm. The blade opened the skin and separated the tissue and muscle as blood poured out from the open wound. She raised her arm to her mouth and licked the wound, then slowly cupped her lips over the blood and sucked with a sick, wet, sucking sound. She lifted her mouth away as blood and saliva formed bands of blood strings until they pulled away and slapped to her chin. "Oh, thank you, Father — thank you."

"Jordan! Where are you going?" There was a call from the small crowd. Jordan was roaming and having fun with her friends, running from bar to bar until they wound up at an outdoor Collective Soul concert around a casino pool.

"I have to pee; I'll be right there," Jordan yelled back. She opened the door to the portable toilet, closed the door, and locked it behind her. It smelled of piss and vomit mixed with alcohol and shit. Jordan unbuttoned and pulled down her jeans. She squatted over the toilet area, careful that her skin did not touch the wet toilet seat. *God! What the hell is wrong with people? Why are they such pigs?* Jordan pulled up her jeans, fastened the button at the top, and looked into the compact mirror provided on the back of the door. She threw her dirty blonde hair back to expose her beautiful face. Her whole life men had hit on her and grabbed at her. She felt tired. She was in debt with no job and wasn't in love with Josh any more. If there was a rock big enough, she would crawl right underneath it. Jordan straightened up, breathed out, and unlatched the lock on the door. She walked outside to breathe in the fresh air. Then she started down the small path that led back to the crowd.

"My, you look delicious."

Jordan turned to look back at who was lurking behind the shadows to see who belonged to the whisper. The hair on the back of her arms stood straight up. With her head down, she walked faster toward the crowd.

"Where are you going in such a hurry, my lovely?" came a robust and soothing voice at a low whisper. She could feel the warm breath from the lips next to her ear.

The shadows engulfed Jordan's body; a frightened tear found its way down her cheek, and when she looked up, Sam was standing in front of her with a straight-lined smile on his lips. He could smell the urine that dripped down from Jordan's panties from her bathroom break.

"Do it, Father," Kaliea said with a joyful tone in her voice.

Sam pulled Jordan close. He placed the dagger's tip between her breasts, right in front of her heart, and slowly pushed the tip inside. It popped through her skin and chest bone, sliding toward Jordan's heart. Blood flowed over Sam's hand as she let out a soft gasp.

"Shh — it will be over soon. Go to sleep now."

Sam pushed the dagger in further; it penetrated her heart. He stopped and held her there with a slight twist. The blood pulled its way up the blade toward the third and final skull.

The blood reached the skull. The thin crimson line found its way to the eye as the tears rolled down both her cheeks. Jordan's eyes glazed over, staring straight into nothing. There was a slight spasm and a small jerk and then she exhaled a long breath and her lifeless body went limp.

Sam pulled the dagger from Jordan's chest and threw her to the ground behind him. Kaliea ran over to the body when it hit the ground. Drool was dripping out of her mouth, mixing with snot running down over her lips.

"Thank you, Father. She's a perfect fit for my collection."

The blood mixed with the other two skulls. One skull, then two skulls, then three skulls moved and twisted. Teeth formed and grew into razor-sharp, needlelike teeth. One by one, they bit deep into and around Sam's forearm, embedding and mixing with his skin and muscle, wrapping around and down his hand. Sam's upper and lower lip curled back; his teeth clenched as the pain ran up his arm. Sam dropped to his knees, holding the pain. "Ugh…" Blood poured down his arm. He bent over in agony.

"Father!" Kaliea screamed with concern. "What's wrong? What's happening?"

Sam's head snapped back. His eyes rolled with a thin white-blue lightning crackling and dancing around them. The white-blue lightning licked its way up Sam's arm toward his neck, then down his body, engulfing every inch. Kaliea dropped the slaughtered pig to the ground and ran over to her father's side.

"Father, what's happening?"

Sam doubled over on his knees and threw himself back, arms outstretched, fists clenched. The white-blue lightning glowed, starting from the center out, and set off a silent boom! Kaliea flew back and slammed into the portable toilet. Sam slumped over and fell to the ground, breathing with short, quick pants.

"Daughter, get us out of here before someone comes to investigate — now."

***

154

Back at the Motel 6 room, Sam lay on the bed, exhausted and in pain. Kaliea sat across the room, staring at him, waiting to see what would happen next.

Sam sat up on the bed and looked down at his hand, which was wrapped in a towel. He slowly unwrapped the bloody towel from his hand. It was sticky and wet and smelled of rotting flesh; he held it up, staring at it with admiration and a smile.

"My god, look at it. It's beautiful," Sam said, smiling. The handle was attached to his right arm, twisting in and out of his skin down to his hand, where he could hold the dagger but not let it go. The dagger was taking on a life of its own as Sam's blood flowed consistently through all three skulls like it was a part of his body. The mouths were moving in unison, trying to speak to him. Sam heard soft multiple whispers and echoes dancing around his ears.

"*Let us out, let us out, we want to kill now. We are free — free.*"

"Don't worry, you will kill, soon, and his name is Cadence — Cadence Mage."

Chapter 17
The End of the Street

Jenny stood at the doorway to Cadence's office.

"Uncle Cade, why are you sitting in the dark?"

"I'm thinking."

"I know you feel bad about Anne, but…"

"Just leave me alone — please." Cadence stared straight ahead, looking into the dark. All the *what if's* were bouncing around in his head. *What if I had moved faster? What if I had jumped between Sam and Anne? I would have come back to life.* Water welled up around his eyes.

Jenny stared ahead with a lot of concern on her face. She heard a customer enter the store; she looked back and slowly closed the door, careful not to make a sound.

Cadence heard the whispers softly fly in and out of his head.

"Is he the one?"

"Yes, he is the one we need to kill."

"He is beautiful."

"I can't wait; please let's do it now."

"He is Cadence Mage — we will kill him soon."

"Shit! Sam got to the last victim. He got the blood needed for the last skull. Meadow, dammit! Where are you?"

***

Cadence went for a walk and ended up at *The End of the Street*. He opened the door and walked in. The smell of smoke, vomit, and old stale beer filled his nostrils. Cadence had not been back here since Heather murdered Chase in front of him. He walked over to the bar, sat down, and asked the bartender for a glass of wine.

"Here you go, honey," said Lacey, the new girl. She seemed older, with heavy lines on her face showing signs of working a lot mixed with drinking and drugs through the years. She seemed like she had been beautiful at one time. Looking at her body, it had held up. Cadence glanced over to his left. An older man was sitting with his head down; it seemed like he was sleeping. Every so often, his head would nod downward in a quick motion. Then he would look awake and stare at his glass of whiskey and mumble something like, "*Mfggfmm why me and my mfggfmm.*"

Cadence glanced over to his right. A couple were arguing loudly. The man wore a T-shirt too tight for his physique; his belly slumped over his belt area. His hair was slicked back, presumably with a Crisco oil-like substance. His nose had a big knob on the end that

157

intertwined with red veins covering the area, same as a drunk would have after drinking for too many years. The nose looked like it would burst blood at any moment. The girl with him looked like she had been beautiful before all the drugs and alcohol took over her life. She wore a tank top with no bra, her nipples protruding slightly through the material. A rod was stabbed through her bottom lip. Her fingers had "FUCK ME NO" tattooed on them. Cadence figured she wasn't smart enough to realize that she didn't have enough fingers to finish, "NOW."

"Harold! Stop it, lower your voice."

"Shut the fuck up! Stop telling me what to do," Harold screamed in her face as he slammed his glass of beer down on the bar, the beer spilling out of the glass. Jodie flinched and put her hand up in front of her face.

"Goddammit, Harold," Jodie said.

Seeing this, Lacey walked over to the couple. "Can you please keep it down, you two? You are disrupting my customers."

"Why don't you shut the fuck up, bitch? Go get me another beer."

"Hey!" Cadence growled at Harold. "You shouldn't talk to her like that. She's the bartender."

"Fuck off! Who the hell are you to tell me what to do? Sit there and drink your girly glass of wine, asshole."

"Stop it, Harold. Why do you always have to get like this when you drink too much?" Jodie said.

Harold was staring at the bar and reached up and backhanded Jodie across the side of her face. She flew off the stool, hitting the ground.

Orange-red lightning danced around Cadence's hand. With a flick of his wrist, Harold's beer glass lifted and flew into his face, breaking his nose as dark crimson splattered all over his cheeks.

"Fuck," Harold screamed. "How the hell did you do that? Goddammit! Agh — you broke my nose."

"You should shut the hell up and stop hitting on your girl," Cadence said while taking a sip of his wine. "Maybe bad things won't happen to you."

Harold jumped off his stool and ran at Cadence, throwing a punch. Cadence moved to his left and grabbed Harold's arm. Lightning shot through Cadence's hand. He twisted and snapped Harold's wrist, then picked him up and threw him into the empty tables and chairs across the room.

The older man quickly nodded his head upward, "What was that *mfggfmm*." Then he set his head back on the bar. Lacey backed up behind the bar with her mouth open.

"Harold!" Jodie screamed. She left her bar stool and ran over to him and put his head in her lap, stroking his hair while wiping the blood away from his face.

"Sweetie, my love, are you all right? Come on, let me get you home." They both got up and stumbled for the door. Jodie turned toward Cadence. "Fuck you; you're an animal!" she screamed.

Cadence chuckled. "Whatever."

"Hey, thanks for that," Lacey said. "The next one is on me."

Cadence looked at Lacey. His eyes were saying "You are welcome," but they showed, "I need time to myself." Although he loved that the next glass of wine was free.

"So — you were friends with the girl who worked here before me. Her name was Chase, right?"

"Yeah, that's right."

"I didn't know her that well. It seemed like everyone here liked her." Lacey didn't catch on to the whole "I need time to myself" concept.

"Yeah, we were friends. She was the best. She liked to listen; I liked that about her."

"So how did you do that? You know, with the glass? You didn't even touch it."

"Ah, yeah, it's an old family thing. You saw that, huh? So, tell me," Cadence said, still looking down at his wine, "do you always talk this much?"

Lacey threw her head back and laughed. "Ah, yeah, I do."

Cadence's phone rang. He saw it was Jenny. Cadence hit the accept button.

"Jenny, is everything OK?"

"Hey, uncle, are you going to swing back by the store? I need you to grab a few things for me."

***

The bar door opened. Sam stepped inside and looked around the place. He smirked and shook his head at the older man with his forehead pressed down on his beer glass, mumbling to himself. Sam walked over and sat next to Cadence.

"So — was that your comic relief outside?" Sam's face had a hint of delight to it.

"Uh, Jenny, I have to go. An asshole just sat down next to me." Cadence tossed the phone on the bar top and grabbed his glass.

"With all the empty seats in the place, you had to pick the one right next to me. What do you want, Sam?"

"What do I want? I would like a friendly conversation, Cadence. How are you and sweet little Jenny doing?"

"I just came here to have a few glasses of wine and mourn someone dear to me, and don't think for a second, I forgot who is responsible."

"Ah, Cade, you took someone dear from me; I only returned the favor. You are lucky it wasn't poor little Jenny or even you."

"Do you think you scare me, Sam? I am stronger and faster than ever, if you haven't noticed, and I won't hesitate to use it."

Sam chuckled and placed his dagger hand on the bar top. It smelled of rotting flesh and oozed pus and blood; the infection was getting worse. Cadence eyed the fused dagger on his arm and let out a long sigh. "Yeah, you should get that looked at."

Lacey walked over to the two. "Can I get you a drink, sir?" She was staring at Sam.

"Please leave us; maybe clean glasses or count your tips. Just — go away," Sam said with an evil stare that made Lacey uncomfortable.

"What do you want, Sam? Can I enjoy my glass of wine without you coming here busting my balls and being rude to the bartender?"

"I'm letting you know I am coming for you."

"So I've heard. What's that all about? Still pissed about the wall, or is it, oh yeah, your dead daughter?" Cadence formed a sarcastic smile on his lips.

Sam gripped the hilt of the dagger tighter in his hand as his top lip curled up, causing blood and pus to ooze onto the bar top and mix with the existing slime that had been there for years; then he heard the whispers.

"*Stop, do not harm or kill Cadence yet. He will be mad.*"

"*Yes, he will be mad.*"

"Your brother — he didn't tell you, did he?"

"Tell me what?" Cadence was losing his patience when Sam mentioned his brother.

"I will make you a deal, Cade. If you come willingly without a fight, I will leave sweet little Jenny alone, and no harm will come to her. Then, you know — she can mourn you after I kill *you*."

"You even think of touching Jenny, you dick, I will make sure you suffer by killing everything and everyone you love before coming for you." Cadence clenched his teeth so hard he thought he had chipped a few.

"Hahaha!" Sam laughed. He slapped his good hand on the bar while holding his new pus-infected hand up. "Well, Cade, this is my exit. Look over your shoulder and make sure your nightmares do not include me."

"Fuck off!" Cadence turned to Sam — but he wasn't there. Cadence shook his head as the bar door closed.

"Man, that guy seems like a real jerk," Lacey said, setting another full glass in front of him.

Cadence chuckled. "Yeah, that's saying it lightly." Cadence lifted the free glass of wine to his lips and sent the first sip through.

Chapter 18
Graves Hassin

Detective Graves Hassin stood leaning against the wall; his face was thin and nerdy, but pretty. Standing five foot eight, with a thin, slinky frame, his hair was dark brown and pushed back down to his shoulders. He seemed a little uncomfortable leaning there on the wall. Graves's shirt was neatly ironed with a flat, one-colored tie. He exposed his detective badge down on his belt, left side, with his firearm sitting on his right front side. He was waiting for someone.

Cadence walked out of *The End of the Street* after a few more glasses of wine. It turned out Lacey was a good listener when you sit around talking and babbling about what's on your mind; she listened to all of his problems with a smile on her face, nodding every few seconds. He got up from his stool and thanked her for her ear and left the bar. Behind him, the neon light turned off, and the door locked. Cadence started down the alley when he stepped into a puddle and splashed water up over his shoes. "Ah, shit, that sucks." Cadence hopped on one foot, thinking it would dry that second. Graves saw Cadence walking away from the bar, coming toward him.

“Are you the one they call Cadence Mage?”

Cadence looked toward the voice. Graves peeled himself off the wall and walked over to him.

Cadence nodded his head. “Yeah, that’s the name my mother gave me. Who is asking?”

“I’m Detective Hassin, Graves Hassin.” He extended his hand out to Cadence; Cadence stared at it for a few moments. Graves blushed with embarrassment and pulled his hand back and set it down by his side.

“I’m investigating the murder of Jordan Greene. Someone stabbed her to death and left her lying in the bushes a few nights ago. They transferred me here down from Montana to help solve these murders that Lieutenant Anne Black worked on.”

“Huh.” Cadence lifted one eyebrow, mouth twisted to the left. “That’s awesome.”

“Yeah, whatever. I’m aware you know of the other two murders. A stab wound to the chest. They haven’t caught the killer,” Graves said.

“Huh, next thing you’ll say is that I was consulting Lieutenant Anne Black with these murders, and now you want me to continue helping you with the same consulting.”

“Something like that. What do you say? Can you help me shed some light on the issue here?”

Cadence’s chest expanded. He held it there for a few seconds and then exhaled slowly.

“Sure. Want to come with me?”

“Where are we going?”

"To my store, so I can… shed some light on your issue for you."

***

The rain came down heavily, cooling off everything that had been exposed and just sitting in the desert heat. Cadence opened the door to the store and walked into the cold air and dryness, with Graves following behind.

Graves looked around the room. It was dim with some lit candles flickering in areas around the store. Dust mites floated in the rays of light all around them. The rows of books were stacked and piled like it had taken years to create the visual effect with the mixture of old and new. There were ancient swords, guns, all types of jewelry, rings, necklaces, and bracelets, with antique lamps, vases, and small furniture from the past. Graves stood there looking around, water dripping off his hair and clothes. He nodded, regarding two women who walked out of the store as their umbrellas popped open to protect them from the raindrops.

"Nice place," Graves said, walking by a desk full of books, swiping his fingers across the surface, disrupting the top layer of dust. He looked at his fingers and, seeing the debris, pulled a tissue from the inside of his sport jacket and wiped his hand. He turned to see a cute girl with milky white skin walking into the room.

"Hey, Uncle Cade!"

Cadence snapped his head at hearing his niece's voice. Jenny stumbled into the room; her toe hit the edge of the carpet, pulling up at the top step.

"Shit! You know, we need to get that fixed." She stared up at Cadence. "Hey — hey." She looked over at Graves. She bounced straight up. "Hi!" Jenny's face went warm as blood rushed to her cheeks and ran red with embarrassment. "Well, Uncle Cade, I have asked you to fix that step for a while now, you know. Can you *please* do something about it?"

"Yea, sure I'll get right on it." Cadence sarcastically chuckled.

"Good." Jenny straightened herself out with a quick nod toward Cadence. "Oh, I almost forgot why I came in here. A new shipment of books arrived, I had them placed in your office. It's getting crowded in there, please go through them and sort them out soon."

"Noted," Cadence looked over at Graves with a crooked smile.

"Can you tell me why we are here and who is this — I don't know — this clumsy girl?" Graves said, looking around the room, sounding a little stuffy and bored. The floor creaked and the walls whispered as the wind blew through them. "What is this place, and is this poor girl a fixture here?"

"This is my niece, Jenny," Cadence snorted.

Cadence walked over to row "H". His finger slid along the spine of the books.

"All right, here it is, *The History of Rare Daggers.*" Cadence walked over to the table and set the book down. He thumbed through the pages until he stopped on page forty-two and slammed his finger on the picture. "You want to know why we are here? That's it."

Graves stared at the picture; in the photo was a dagger. The blade had three grooved lines from the tip leading straight up to the handle, and it had three skulls back-to-back. The grooves led to each skull.

"Well, that's unique," Graves said, staring down at the book with a bewildered expression. "So, why are you showing me this?"

"Well, this is your murder weapon. This dagger killed all three girls. Once it's had the blood of three young girls, it spreads and directs the blood to all three heads. Then the dagger chooses a host and embeds itself into the arm of the host. It then allows the host to control all the souls the dagger murdered and collected through the years. The host becomes The Eyes for the Souls."

"This shit sounds like it's straight out of an *Indiana Jones* movie. Come on, you don't expect me to believe this crap, do you?"

"No, I do not. I am showing you what Anne and I were researching before her murder. She didn't believe me either. So — you sure you want to keep pursuing this investigation? How far do you want to go with this?"

Graves thought for a moment and nodded his head at Cadence. "I'm all in, Mr Mage." Graves pushed his chair back. It scraped across the floor as he stood up. "Where do we start?"

"We start by not calling me Mr Mage; it's Cadence." Cadence closed the book and turned to put it back on the shelf, when Jenny poked her head in the door.

"Hey, Uncle Cade? You have a minute?" Her eyes shifted over to Graves.

***

A few hours later, after sitting down with Cadence while he explained who he was and the importance of finding the dagger and what had happened to Anne, Graves sat there trying to understand.

The door closed behind Graves as he left the store; Graves set a crooked smile on his face, shook his head, and walked down the alley.

"Is he the one?"

"We want to kill him."

"We need to kill him—"

Graves stopped, swiped at his ear, and looked into the mystery of the air, wondering why he heard voices.

"No — he's not the one."

"We can't kill him."

"Leave him be."

Graves smiled a crooked smile again and kept walking. His whistling was faint with a slight echo bouncing off the alley walls until he disappeared into the shadows.

Chapter 19
Jenny Mage

There was a loud bang! Jenny shot straight up in her bed. Her hair was all spiked up and going in all directions. Her bottom lip stuck out and blew a breath upward to move a few strands of hair from her face. "What the hell was that?" Jenny said out loud to herself.

Jenny peeled the covers back and swung her legs over the side of the bed. She stood and walked into the kitchen.

Her one-bedroom apartment was old, with worn-down wooden floors that creaked with every step she took. It was a hot night, and the room was dimly lit; she lived right above the store for the convenience. She opened the refrigerator. The light lit up the room. She grabbed a Starbucks in a can and sat down at the table with Graves on her mind. He was cute and nerdy and goofy, and she couldn't stop thinking about him.

"Hello, Jenny." The voice felt like it was pulling from her thoughts. A blue-purple flame formed in front of Jenny and moved toward her face.

"The niece of Cadence. My — you are beautiful."

Jenny was trembling, and she could not move. Her Starbucks still sat on the table. She wanted to reach over and grab it and take a big gulp from it. Instead, she stared deep into the blue-purple flame; she could see gray rotting teeth, with horns and blood running down into a smile.

"*Like what you see, little Jenny?*"

"No, no, I don't!" She shook her head. "Why… why would I like what I see? You are disgusting. Who are you, and what are you?"

"*Your father, Jenny. Oh, how clever Christopher thinks he is, killing himself so he could find mommy and pull her back.*"

"Wait, you're telling me that dad… Uncle Cade told me—"

"*Uncle Cade — oh, little Jenny, Cadence and his brother thought they could outsmart me!*" The blue-purple flame laughed and spread further into the room.

"You are that strange flame my uncle keeps talking about," Jenny said with a quiver, her voice shaking and with terror in her eyes. "You are the one who took my grandmother."

"*I so wanted to meet you, Jenny, oh, and I do like you. There is darkness in you that's compelling. I can feel it; it's strong in you, and in time you will learn to use your gifts. For now, can you be my little messenger for me? I want you to tell Cadence the dagger is complete. It will release the souls, including my soul, and soon we will all be whole again. Then Cadence will finally understand who I am. Oh, tell your uncle that*

172

Christopher has failed to find their mother. The little plan they dreamed up was a waste of time."

The coldness of the room warmed. The sound of the refrigerator broke the dead silence. Jenny glanced over toward the window. She saw the last bit of the blue-purple flame die out.

Jenny sat there; she blew out a long breath, thinking of her dad. She reached over and grabbed the Starbucks can, opened it, and quickly drank it.

Jenny sat there until morning, peeking through the blinds. She thought to herself, *What does he mean? There is darkness in me? And what's the little plan between my dad and uncle?* She slowly got up and went to the bathroom, showered, and slipped into her clothes. Jenny grabbed her keys and walked down the stairs to unlock the store and wait for her uncle.

***

Cadence sat at his desk, sighed, and went through the mail piled up on top. Another new shipment of junk. He picked up a book, turned it over front to back, and then threw it on the table. Dust flew up around the corners of the book. *Not like they used to be*, Cadence thought. The room was quiet, more than usual. Cadence had this slight buzzing sound roaming through his ears. He heard the click sound as the front door unlocked into place, then the sound of small feet coming down the hallway toward his office, then a slight rapping on the door.

"Uncle Cade, you in there?"

"No, please go away!"

The door slowly opened; oil was needed.

"Unc, we need to talk."

"Jenny, I'm really not in the mood."

"Well, you need to get in the mood. Does a blue-purple flame remind you of anything?"

Cadence's head quickly popped up to look at Jenny. "What did you say?" Cadence was caught with a surprise expression on his face; it gradually turned into a worried look. "What's going on, Jenny?"

"Can you please listen to me?"

"Jen! What the hell?"

"Uncle — shut up! Will you just shut up for one second, dammit!" Jenny stamped her foot on the wood-planked floor and crossed her arms with anger that settled into her emotions.

Cadence stopped with confusion circling his face. "OK, jeez! You don't have to yell this early in the morning."

Jenny calmed herself before she explained. "The blue-purple flame said he wanted you to know the—"

"Yes, I know; the dagger is complete," Cadence interrupted Jenny.

"He also said that the souls are almost complete, including his."

Cadence stared hard.

"What do you mean, including his? Oh! Shit, I didn't see this one coming." Cadence stood up and walked over, removed the cover to the eye of the shrunken head, and the stairs descended. Cadence hurried inside with Jenny close behind.

Cadence looked around his bookshelves.

"Uncle Cade, did you and dad, um, plan his death together?"

Cadence turned to Jenny. His mouth was open. "Huh? What?"

"Did you and dad plan his death? Please tell me what's going on. What did you do?" Tears started welling up in Jenny's eyes.

"Got it!" Cadence yelped with excitement. He walked over to the podium and slammed the book down. The title read *Ancient Daggers and Their Creators.* Cadence looked over at Jenny, tears falling from her face.

"Oh, Jenny, I'm sorry; I got so wrapped up in finding this book, I wasn't listening to you. Here, Jenny, sit right here."

Jenny slumped down in the chair that Cadence was holding out for her. She wiped the tears from her face and stared up at him. Cadence let out a heavy sigh. He sat down on the corner of the desk and stared at Jenny.

"OK — yes, Jenny, your dad and I planned his death. Your dad, well, he was hell-bent on finding your grandmother. He had this over-the-top idea about finding her and pulling her back." Cadence stood up and walked over to the wine cabinet. He set a glass down and poured a red. He swirled the glass so the wine could breathe and activate all the aromas. Then he put the glass to his lips and tasted the sweet berries on his tongue.

"I didn't like the idea." Cadence stared at the dark metal statue sitting in the corner. "Christopher was excited, and he was sure his plan would work. Hell, he even had me convinced, after a while; but something kept eating at me. Now you're telling me that the blue-purple flame came to visit you last night. Something is off here. He must have discovered our plan. Either your dad didn't think this through, or the blue-purple flame was expecting this to happen."

"So, what was my dad thinking? That he would just kill himself and outsmart the blue-purple flame?"

"Well," Cadence said, rubbing the back of his neck, "funny you should ask. I'm guessing he thought he would die by the dagger and look for our mother and wait for his soul to become whole again. Then he would pull her back through the darkness with him. He never told me how, but now I think I know how."

"So, you weren't with him when he died?"

"No, I wasn't. Christopher told me he wanted to do that alone." Cadence was looking down at the book while flipping through the pages. "Here, I showed a watered-down version of this to that Detective Graves."

Jenny's head snapped up at the sound of Graves's name. Cadence brought the book over to Jenny. She stared at the page he showed her. It showed a painting of hundreds of souls flying around a three-headed dagger, each face more evil, than the next. There, in the center of the souls, was a figure. It was powerful-looking, with red-orange scales and horns protruding out of each side of its head.

"Tidus Brack." His fingers landed on the name. "Page six hundred and sixty-six." The description read: "*Tidus Brack, King of the Abyss, High Chancellor of Hell Who Tends to Satan.*"

"OK — I guess the fun stops!" Jenny stood. Goosebumps formed all over her arms. "So, who is this blue-purple flame?"

"That's him, Tidus Brack. He is… the blue-purple flame."

"So, you're saying that dad knew this all along?"

"No." Cadence looked down, shaking his head. "That's just it. I don't think he knows who Tidus Brack is, but what's baffling me is how Christopher knew about the three-headed dagger. Tidus is the dagger's creator. He knew that one day this dagger would help him find his way back to this world."

"All right, why?"

"Let's go find out. Come on." Cadence walked out and closed the door to the secret room; Jenny followed.

"Where are we going?" Walking through the hallway toward the front of the store, Jenny turned to her uncle with one eyebrow up.

"We have to find Meadow."

"Meadow, the witch?" Graves asked; both Cadence and Jenny turned toward the front door, where Graves was standing.

"Shit, where did you come from?" Cadence was startled as he almost ran into Graves. Jenny looked all bashful, looking down while shifting her eyes up to meet his.

"Is it OK if I come along for the ride?"

"Sure, more the merrier, but don't talk; just stand there and look pretty." Cadence slapped his hand on Graves's shoulder and walked past him and out through the store's entrance. Jenny followed him with her head down, avoiding eye contact.

Chapter 20
Discovered

Meadow's voice started as a whisper in Cadence's head as he stood in the cemetery in front of Anne's headstone.

"So, I think you miss me, Cady, and I see you brought your friends with you." Slowly, a figure appeared in front of Cadence. Jenny and Graves stood there, staring at her. She wore a long flowing dress that hugged her curves. It was a soft fabric, white with a yellow daisy pattern, that rested on the top of her feet. Her hair was long, a strawberry blonde color cropped shorter on the sides. She was beautiful. Detective Graves kept staring at her. Jenny looked up at him with a slightly angry expression. Graves turned to her, looked away, and then back again; he swallowed hard and loud. Jenny, satisfied with the outcome, turned her attention back to Cadence and Meadow.

"Are you ready for my father, Cade? I warned you he was coming."

"Yeah, yeah, I know you did. The cemetery seems like the only spot you will meet me, but nevertheless. Have you heard of someone named Tidus Brack?"

"Father mentioned him once or twice; heard him say he was the key person in his little crusade in killing

you. From what I gather, this plan has been in the works for thousands of years." Meadow's voice floated through all their heads like a dream in a heavy sleep. A breeze blew through and sent hot air like a hairdryer across Cadence's face. There, stood Kaliea.

"I knew you were feeding Cadence information and stabbing Father in the back, you bitch!" Kaliea ran at Meadow, but she ran right into black smoke as Meadow evaporated. Kaliea turned with confusion on her face and looked at Cadence.

"You did this. This is all your fault. You need to die. My sister is still in love with you, and you just took advantage of that once again, didn't you?" Kaliea pulled lightning through her hands and shot them toward Cadence. Cadence moved slightly to his right. The lightning hit the tree behind him and sent bark flying. Standing next to the tree was Jenny. Graves grabbed her and threw her out of harm's way as he fell on top of her. Kaliea dropped to her knee. Cadence reached down, grabbed her by the hair at the back of her head, and pulled her head back. He then bent her face down and gave her a right uppercut. Kaliea flew backward in the air and came slamming down on top of the headstone marked "Anne Black". Kaliea stood up laughing, wiping blood from her mouth and straightening her crooked bones.

"Hahaha, you just hit a lady, you bad boy."

"Really — you, a lady? Have you passed by a mirror lately, you ugly bitch?"

Kaliea had just brushed herself off when Cadence kicked her high in the chest. She flew back again about ten feet, then she hit the ground. Tendrils of lightning wrapped around her body; she arched up, screaming. Cadence stood there, staring at Meadow; her hands were outstretched toward Kaliea. The blue, thin lightning tendrils seemed like extensions of her hands, wrapping all around Kaliea.

Graves looked up at the scene unfolding in front of him, his mouth open.

"Hello! Excuse me." Jenny stared up at Graves. He was standing over Jenny. "You think maybe you can, I don't know, help me up?"

Graves stared down at her. "Oh, right — sorry." Feeling a little embarrassed, he reached down, grabbed her hand, and pulled her up onto her feet.

"Thank you," Jenny said with a half-smile on her lips, brushing herself off.

"You know, sister, you are becoming sloppy and careless." Meadow squeezed the tendrils tighter as she backed up slowly. Kaliea was laughing while standing.

"Little sister, you are still not strong enough to best me." The tendrils dropped and disappeared from around her. "What do you think, Father? Is she worthy yet?"

Sam stepped out from the shadow of the trees. "Meadow, where have you been, my child? Tell me, why have you been conspiring with Cadence against me?" Sam spoke with soft anger in his voice. "You disappoint me, my daughter."

"What, I disappoint you?" Meadow shot back.

"Child!" Sam cut Meadow short.

"No, Father, you have disappointed me! You praise Kaliea and Heather. Why? Because you still hold me responsible for Mother's death. She was teaching me the dark magic. I didn't mean to kill her — why can't you see that? I was young and didn't know any better."

"Oh, shut up with all your pathetic excuses. You know you are responsible for Mother's death and no one else," Kaliea said.

"Enough!" Sam yelled. Kaliea backed away, her head down. "We need to get back to our business, and Meadow, you are coming with me. So, say goodbye to your friends and come over here and stand next to me."

"Meadow — you don't have to go with him; stay here, with me. They don't care about you; all they want is to keep you from telling the truth of what's going on." Cadence held out his hand for her to take.

"Meadow, now! Cadence, you and I will settle our matters soon, but not today," Sam said, with black smoke lingering around his tall figure. "So, stay out of our family business and stay away from my daughter."

"You stay away from my uncle, you fucking sleazy, slimy — pig!" Jenny held up her fuck-you finger as her last words trailed off by the stare that Sam gave her. She danced around and stood behind Graves.

"Jenny," Cadence barked, "let me handle this."

"There is nothing to handle, Cade. In three days, I will handle you; and little Jenny, aren't you the brave one?" The black smoke thickened around Sam and the girls. "Three days, Cade. If you try to hide, I will find you."

"Don't worry, I won't be hiding. I'll make sure it's easy to find me." Cadence smirked at Sam and then looked at Meadow as she disappeared. All she could do was silently mouth, *I am sorry.*

As the black smoke surrounded them, Kaliea stared at Cadence. "He, he, he, three days." With a big smile on her face, she disappeared.

"Now, what the hell just happened?" Graves asked, while standing with his gun drawn and a confused look on his face.

"What happened, Graves, is that's the person responsible for killing the girls and Anne with the dagger and trying to set the souls free, so they can come and kill me."

Graves stared at Cadence, not saying a word.

"So — are you in?" Cadence said.

"I don't know what I'm getting myself into, but, yeah, sure I'm in."

"Great! Jenny, Graves, we have a lot to do in the next three days, so let's get to it. Jenny — 'sleazy, slimy pig', really? Hahaha." Cadence laughed and walked toward the cemetery entrance.

Chapter 21
Tidus Brack

Thousands of years ago, they considered Tidus Brack a god of all men. He was an evil god, doing heinous acts of violence that made humans cower and hide when he walked by. They marked Tidus as a killer of women and children, who loved to torture and mutilate his prey. One day the underworld took notice of his violent acts among the humans. The king of the underworld called upon Tidus to meet with him in his chambers.

"Ah, so you are the one they call Tidus, the killer and torturer of women and children."

Tidus stood there, very proud and egotistical, looking around the king's chamber. Its enormous walls were black and looked like they were moving with souls intertwining with other souls, weaving in and out of each other, and in the center back against a wall was the king, sitting on his concrete throne, engulfed by the dark shadows. Tidus could not see his face or body. The only exposed parts were the king's hands, and by his side was a large sword. The blade was black as night, yet sparkled when the light hit it just right. Halfway up the blade were human skulls on top of skulls. They wrapped around the grip, with one last skull mounted to form the top of the pommel. Tidus nodded at the question with a smile.

"I am, my king of the underworld." Tidus bowed and appeared proud, standing in front of his king. "So, what is the nature of this meeting you ask of me, my king?"

"I have a proposition for you, Tidus," a low, deep, bellowing voice said. "I would like you to leave the humans and come here to do my bidding, as the keeper of my world that watches over it."

The quest asked of Tidus made him smile with delight. Upon his acceptance of this role, decades and centuries passed, but no one was more loyal to the king than Tidus. The king grew weary and bored with Tidus and his loyalty, so the king had some fun testing his loyalty. The king grabbed a young maiden chosen from the humans. She was vibrant and headstrong; she even worshipped the black magic. So the king appointed her as Tidus's personal servant, but was told by the king he was never to touch her for pleasure.

Her name was Isabella Mage. She was strikingly beautiful, like a goddess herself. Through the passing time, Tidus fell deeply in love with Isabella. All he dreamed and thought about was Isabella and her smile; and, in time, she fell in love with Tidus. Through the years, they would both meet in a hidden secret chamber of the main hall and make love all night, and in the morning they would both sneak off and go to their separate rooms.

When the news got back to the king about the two, he smiled, then ran his sword through the messenger, starting at his belly and up through his head. He threw the messenger to the ground as his myth hounds crawled over and feasted on his flesh, tearing and ripping at the innards while they slipped, fell, and wriggled around in the wet sticky blood.

Tidus stood before the king, nervous, and not knowing why the king had summoned him.

"You disappoint me, Tidus," the king bellowed.

"What do you mean, my king? Have I not always been loyal to you? Have I not pleased you?"

"Don't think me a fool!" the king yelled, his voice deep and hard. "You disobeyed my orders, and now you stand here before me and cast all these lies my way!" The king reached down from his throne, grabbed Tidus by his neck, and lifted him off the ground. He pulled him close to his face. "Now you will pay the consequences for your deceiving actions."

Tidus found himself on his knees and in shackles, his arms up high, and his head bowed down in shame.

"My king, I am sorry, please forgive me. I did not mean to be so disloyal to you. Can't you find mercy in your heart for someone so loyal?"

"Stop!" the king bellowed. "You will remain in these chains until I say otherwise."

Years passed. Tidus remained in the shackles and on his knees. One day, he opened his eyes to find Isabella in front of him, tears streaming down her face.

"I am so sorry, Tidus, my love. Please forgive me? I didn't mean to." She was shaking with fright.

"You didn't mean to what, Isabella?" Tidus said.

The king was standing behind Isabella and grabbed her by the back of the neck and held her up.

"She belongs to me now — don't you, Isabella?" The king laughed.

Days fell into weeks that fell into decades and then centuries. The king kept beating and raping Isabella repeatedly as he forced Tidus to watch. Each time he raped her, Tidus's anger grew.

"Why are you doing this, my king?" Tidus said with heavy remorse, only to watch it happen. The flesh on his wrists were sliced into by the cold, heavy steel shackles that wrapped around them. The flesh flapped over the steel while the shackles pulled tighter and tighter as he screamed and jerked his body while being forced to repeatedly watch the woman he loved being humiliated, raped, and beaten for decades and centuries. All the while, the king laughed with delight.

Tidus hung there for so long he couldn't feel himself or his soul any more. All he could do was watch Isabella being treated like this — an endless loop of horror with tears and pain.

***

When Isabella had her first child, she named the boy Christopher. He was a beautiful child. Tidus screamed at hearing the news. The second child she named Cadence. The king stood tall, chest out, boasting in front of Tidus.

"So now I can finally bring all this fun to an end, Tidus. I can finally let you die."

Tidus's head lay low, still on his knees. He slowly looked up at his king, and all he whispered was, "*Thank you, my king*," crying from exhaustion.

The king bent down so he was face-to-face with Tidus.

"I think I will kill you with the gift you gave me. It fits beautifully in my hand." He slowly slid the dagger's blade into Tidus's heart and whispered into his ear, "*Loyalty never mattered.*" The king laughed.

The dagger was made of black metal; it had three etched lines that led up to the pommel. There were three skulls, back-to-back, made of human bone. The dagger had been created by Tidus's hands and given to the king as a gift. He had known that his death would come by the king's hands one day, but what he did not tell the king was that he added an enchanted spell on the dagger. Whoever's life the dagger took would hold the soul behind the skulls' eyes until someone used it to kill three young girls. So, the dagger could use their blood to release the souls and make them whole again. He called it The Eyes for the Souls.

Chapter 22
Souls: Part One

The dagger slammed into the stone. One by one, the wormlike tentacles squirmed and moved under the skin. Then they pulled away from underneath the muscle, leaving dark holes bleeding. Sam cried out in pain and stared down at the dagger. Disappointed, he saw it wasn't a part of him anymore.

"It's almost time," Sam screamed out.

"Oh, Father, this is so exciting. I want Cadence to beg on his knees right before you kill him."

Sam's fingers lightly danced around the dagger as thin white lightning licked at his fingers and around the skulls.

"It won't be long now; I can feel it. They're coming." Sam threw his arms out and his head back, while white lightning wrapped around his body and soul.

"You don't want to let this happen, Father. Killing Cadence will only cause havoc to us all. Why are you so obsessed with him?" Meadow begged and pleaded with her father.

"Why, my young naïve sister, it turns out that Cadence's father is none other than Satan, the king of the underworld. Once he is dead, we will wear all his powers!" said Kaliea.

"What? He never mentioned this before," Meadow said.

"That's because he does not know. That's why I am so excited. I want to see his face when Father tells him."

***

Cadence, Jenny, and Graves were driving in Graves's car. They were heading toward nowhere. All they were doing was following Cadence's erratic directions. As whispers danced around his ears, they were telling him where to go.

"We will kill you."

"You are the one."

"We now know you are the demon hunter."

The voices kept going in and out of his left and right ear.

"The old church—"

"In the center—"

"The broken church—"

"In the desert—"

"The walls speak to us."

Cadence kept telling them where to go. Jenny and Graves listened as he took them deep into the desert. Up ahead, Graves saw a faint light.

"Hey, over there, I see lights."

"That's where we are going; just head that way." Cadence shook his head to break away the whispers from his ears.

Slowly, they pulled the car forward. A single vehicle was sitting outside, its lights shining toward the old broken church. Two of the four remaining walls had fallen. The paint was faded and peeled back off the walls, with dust caked over them and piled-up bricks at the base of the walls. Half of the steeple on the roof had snapped off and was lying on the ground. All the stained-glass windows had been blown out, either from a rock being thrown through them or from the heavy desert winds, sending shards of glass everywhere.

"Sam is in there, along with Kaliea and Meadow." Cadence opened the car door and stepped out.

"What are we going to do?" Jenny sounded a little excited.

"You, Jenny, will stay here in the car." Graves looked in Jenny's direction.

"Oh, hell no, I want to kick the shit out of that ugly ass witch bitch Kaliea."

"Jenny! Stay in the car for me, please," Cadence barked.

"This sucks!" Jenny slumped back into the seat and folded her arms.

"Graves, you have your guns?"

"Oh — you betcha I do."

"Good, let's go."

Graves stepped out of the car and they both walked toward the broken church. The night was hot and dry, with no wind anywhere. Not a sound could be heard except for the crackling of the fires burning at the four corners of the church and the one at the center where the stone podium stood with the dagger sticking out of it. Cadence and Graves walked into the open area.

"Hi, everyone, I'm here! Now the party can begin, isn't that right, Kaliea?"

Kaliea backed up and stood behind her father. Meadow glared over at her with a smile, excited to see Cadence. Sam still stared down at the dagger in the stone, with more lightning building up through his hand and licking around, weaving in and out of the three skulls surrounding the blade.

"*What's happening?*" Graves whispered in Cadence's ear, his eyes wide, staring at what was happening around the center of the broken church.

"I'm not sure, but I am about to find out." Cadence built up lightning in his arms; when they reached his hands, he shot them out with fingers spread. The bolts shot forward at Sam. Sam swiped his left hand and batted the bolts harmlessly away. He slammed them across the broken church, where the lightning hit the back wall and fizzled away.

From the corner of the church, slowly coming up from the fire, stood a shape. It waddled out of the flames as if both of its feet were broken at the ankles. It was still on fire, making crackling and popping noises. As the fire slowly burned away, Cadence stared at the shape. It was slimy, with a gray skin tone color. The skin was falling off its skeletal frame, like it was wearing a coat too big for its body. Its face looked like it was melting and falling off its skull's frame. It made a low growl, like a gurgling whisper.

"Now, I kill Cadence."

A second shape followed up out of the fire. Then, across the room in another corner, two more creatures emerged from the fire. Then two more from the other corner. Eight creatures had emerged from the flames, all whispering the same thing over and over.

"Kill Cadence, kill Cadence."

Rising from the fire at the center of the church was the blue-purple flame. Melting within, a shape formed. It was the large form of a man with skin covered in red-orange scales. As he stood, smoke formed all around him. Horns grew out to two to three feet high from each side of his head. His nose was missing, with only two slits in place, with slime dripping down out of each opening. Every tooth was razor-sharp, top and bottom, accompanied by another row behind the first. Saliva poured down from the middle of its bottom lip.

"Ah! It feels great to be alive again. I can feel the night air all around me." Tidus stood there. Eyes closed, arms outstretched, he took a deep breath while admiring dozens of shadow demons running along the broken church. Shadow demons were made of moving shadows. Their arms were longer than their bodies, the fingers extended and extremely sharp, which helped them move quickly and cling to walls and ceilings or any other surface. They were pitch black, with large heads and without eyes. Their skin was stretched tightly wrapped around the bones. They had pure white razor-sharp teeth with the two front ones longer than the rest, like a vampire.

Tidus opened his eyes and looked around to soak up the surroundings of the broken church. Then his eyes fell on Cadence.

"Cadence, it's good to see you again. I am so glad you are here. Please, don't make this any harder for yourself, you humans — you just stink of the living, and I fucking hate that smell."

"Yeah, yeah, that flame suited you better, or whatever the hell you were. I will not make this easy for you, and you can bet on that."

"Cadence, death does not run. It stops only to embrace. Tonight, you will learn this."

Cadence stood, staring up at Tidus, his legs slightly apart, arms and hands down, palms out. Sliding down from Cadence's sleeve was Ethereal; his hand gripped the handle. Lightning danced around the other hand, as he stepped forward and shot his arm out. A stream of lightning shot forward and wrapped around Tidus. He stood there, unfazed by the lightning. Tidus reached out his hands to the lightning, pulled it off like a piece of clothing, and threw it at the wall. The impact exploded and shook the remaining walls around the broken church. Dust flew around. Tidus laughed.

"You poor boy, you don't even know how to use the gifts your father gave you," Tidus bellowed.

Cadence twirled his sword and spun to his left. He sliced through the head of the shadow demon standing closest to him, straight down the middle, and split it apart; brains and blood slapped the concrete floor. He spun completely around and separated two more demons' heads from their bodies as they hit the concrete and rolled, then stopped in front of Tidus's feet.

Tidus held his right hand out and formed it into a fist, then quickly opened his fingers. Cadence was lifted off the ground. Tidus threw him across the room, smashing him into two of the slimy creatures in the corner.

The first slimy creature grabbed Cadence and lifted him by his throat. A gunshot rang out. The bullet hit the shape in the back of the head, exploding the front of its skull, with brains and dark blood slapping Cadence in the face. The creature fell to its knees and then disintegrated into the air like burnt ash. Everyone looked over at Graves. He stood there, smoking gun pointed forward. Kaliea shot a bolt of lightning at Graves. He fell and rolled to his left; the bolt flew past him and exploded against the decayed wall behind him. Graves stood up, pointed, and pulled the trigger on the second creature standing next to Cadence. The skull exploded and painted the wall behind it a dark crimson color. The brains rolled slowly down the brick wall, mixing with dirt and dust on the way down. All Cadence could do was nod back at Graves and think to himself, *Glad I brought him along.*

Kaliea disappeared and then reappeared right behind Graves. She had grabbed him around the neck from behind, when a wooden two-by-four smacked Kaliea in the back of her head. Kaliea screamed as she fell to her knees. She turned and looked up. There was Jenny.

"Get your slimy hands off him, you ugly motherfucker." She swung the wood stick again and hit Kaliea across the face, spinning her around.

"No!" Sam cried out. He flew toward Jenny and backhanded her across the face, sending her to the ground.

"Agh!" Graves swung and punched Sam across the jaw, sending him backward, falling on his backside, and then fired two shots at him, but Sam disappeared before the bullets arrived. Graves ran over to Jenny.

"You all right?" Graves had a worried look in his eyes.

Jenny smiled. "This… is going to be fun."

***

On the other side of the broken church, Tidus flicked his wrist at Cadence and slammed him into the brick wall. His head hit hard and left a small circle of blood. Tidus flicked his wrist again; Cadence flew and slammed into a half-broken statue, face-first. Blood covered his face. He rolled, stopping at Tidus's feet. Tidus reached down with his massive horns. He picked up the bloody, wounded, and delirious Cadence through his shirt and brought them face-to-face.

"Humans always look so frightened. How I have waited for thousands of years for this very moment. Thank your father for this, Cadence. He tortured me, beat me, and repeatedly raped and beat the one I loved for thousands of years, and now it is my turn. I will kill the one precious thing he loves: his favorite son, Cadence. I will kill you slowly so I can hear his faint cries deep from below the earth."

Cadence hung there, swinging back and forth, blood dripping from his nose and mouth. Jenny was kicking and screaming as one of the slimy creatures was about to grab her and rip her head from her body. Graves stepped on the two-by-four. It flipped up and he grabbed one end of it and smacked the gray shape square in the face; it flew back and hit the ground. Graves turned the two-by-four stick and slammed it down edge first into the slimy creature's skull, right between the eyes and forehead. It ran through clean to the back of the cranium and flattened out on the concrete floor. He repeated this, another five times — and then six, and then seven, until the face was unrecognizable. He stepped back dropping the blood-soaked wooden stick.

"Behind you!" Jenny yelled out, pointing at Graves. As he turned, he pointed his two pistols and pulled the triggers one by one. Hitting the fourth creature in the head and torso, he sent it flying back off its feet and hitting the brick wall, where it lay limp, and then it just disintegrated to burnt ash like the others.

"What... do you mean... my father?" Cadence slurred his words as he spoke.

"You fool! You don't even know who your own father is! No one ever told you?" laughed Kaliea. She was standing next to Tidus. Tidus turned and backhanded her. Her head whipped around as she fell to one knee.

"Don't speak, woman! Just tend to the others that you and your pathetic father are having a hard time defeating," bellowed Tidus.

Kaliea held the side of her face. It felt like it was gone. She got up and ran across the broken church until she was behind her father.

"It's time for you to know the truth, boy! Your father was my king, the king of the underworld. Here on earth, people call him Satan!" screeched Tidus.

"So... let me get this straight. All this mayhem and destruction is because you idiots are convinced that Satan is my father? How ridiculous does that sound? What the hell are you talking about?" Cadence tried to laugh, but choked instead.

Tidus pulled Cadence free from his horns.

"You should not talk about my king like that, boy!" More fury and rage poured from Tidus as he slammed Cadence down, face-first again, into the stone wall. Cadence thought he heard bones breaking inside.

From the far dark corner of the broken church, a figure stepped forward.

"Hello, brother. Hello, Tidus."

Chapter 23
Souls: Part Two

Christopher walked out from the shadows.

"Chris? You asshole!" Cadence was in pain and was annoyed that Chris took so long to show up.

"Dad?" Jenny looked over at her father.

"Jenny, honey, stay where you are. Please don't come any closer."

Jenny stopped moving toward her father.

A slimy creature reached out and grabbed at Christopher. Christopher turned and took hold of the gross beast by the neck with one hand, then picked it up and slammed it to the ground. He then stood over the creature. His hands formed into iced lightning as he shot them down right through the creature's face, causing it to turn and float away into black ash. Cadence stared at his brother, not believing what he just saw.

"How did you do that?"

Christopher stared at his brother and smiled. "Brother, someone here wants to say hello."

Stepping from the shadows behind Christopher, with a slight glow emanating around her, was the most beautiful woman Cadence had ever seen. She had long flowing gray hair and the face of an angel; he thought all that was missing was the wings to complete her.

"Mother?" Cadence stood without taking his eyes off his mother, afraid because she might not really be standing in front of him.

"Isabella!" Tidus was confused at seeing his only true love and walked toward her, not caring about Cadence any more.

"Cadence, my son," Isabella said with tears falling from her face. "Oh, how I've missed you so much." Isabella walked past Tidus straight to Cadence. She put her arms around her youngest son and held him close.

"What happened to you, Mom? Where did you go?" Cadence felt like a young boy again in his mother's arms.

"Tidus, he held me prisoner in the darkness all these years. I tried to get back to you and your brother, but couldn't break the spell. It surprised me when Christopher found me and pulled me back through the dark."

"We searched for you for over a hundred years, Mom. We never stopped."

"I know, my sweet boy. I know you haven't stopped. I love you and your brother so much." Isabella pulled back. "Let me look at you — my, how you've grown into a handsome man. Your brother told me you had a lazy eye and bumps all over your face, but I didn't believe him one bit."

Cadence rolled his eyes, shaking his head. Christopher walked over to his brother and grabbed him in a bear hug, lifted him, and whispered into his ear, "*It's all going to work out, little brother. Mom has a plan.*"

Sam and Kaliea stood there, staring at all the drama playing out in front of them, not knowing Tidus's next move. This was all unexpected.

"Grandmother?" Jenny stood there, staring at this beautiful woman even angels would envy. She glanced over at Graves, his mouth open and eyes glazed over.

"Hey, you, check your eyes — she is my grandmother. Gross!"

Graves turned to Jenny with a crooked smile across his lips.

"My child, you must be Jenny," Isabella said.

"You know my name?"

"Yes, I do; your father has told me all about you. You are every bit as beautiful and more."

Jenny flew over and hugged her father tight, not caring that he had told her to stay where she was. Christopher held her for a moment, then pulled her close and whispered in her ear, "*Please, Jenny, go to the corner of the church and take your boyfriend with you.*"

"He's not—"

"We will talk about this later." He kissed her forehead, and then he pushed her toward a safe location.

Tidus pleaded, "Isabella, please forgive me. I was feeling a lot of hate; I wasn't myself. I was in a rage of jealousy at what my king did to us — did to you. It was the only way I knew how to keep you safe. I need my plan to work so I can defeat the king. I'm doing this for us."

"Oh, Tidus, please change out of that hideous form. You know I always hated when you looked like that; I fell in love with your human form, not that one."

"Anything to please you, my love."

Tidus's face contorted and twisted slightly. His horns slowly descended into his head until they disappeared; his face chiseled out and formed to perfection. There stood a tall, beautiful man, so perfect everyone stared at him and Isabella. They made the ideal lovers. Graves tilted his head, looking over at Jenny. She blushed, staring at the beautiful man, and quickly looked away.

Tidus walked over to Isabella and wrapped his arms around her. He engulfed her in his massive arms. Isabella soothed him and stroked the back of his head. Without hesitation, she grabbed Tidus, spun him around, and pushed him forward. Christopher was standing right behind him with the three-headed dagger he had pulled from the stone while everyone was staring at Tidus and Isabella. Christopher pushed the blade forward, straight through Tidus's heart, then twisted the blade. As the pain shot through Tidus's body, he screamed.

"No! Isabella — what have you done? Why… why do you betray me, but again? I need to kill the king so we can go back to our lives and be happy like before."

Forming up from the ground, swirling around Tidus, a light-blue flame licked around his body, making its way up to the top of his head. It glowed with a light purple color. It swirled around, building up a force faster and faster until all they could now see was a blue-purple flame. Flickering in the center was Tidus's pure form, horns and all, screaming.

"No! No, Isabella, I love you — please! Why are you doing this?" With a silent boom, he was gone. The dagger fell to the ground, clanking back and forth until it finally stood still.

Christopher bent down, picked it up, and handed the dagger to his mother. She gracefully took it, slid it in a soft blue velvet bag, and pulled the small ropes to tighten and secure the opening. She then pushed the bag under her cloak for safekeeping.

Sam became enraged at what he saw. Centuries of planning had been ruined. He ran at Christopher and grabbed him by the throat. Christopher didn't have time to react as they both flew across the church. Christopher slammed into the wall and fell to the ground. Sam slammed his fist down, punching him once, twice, again and again, four times. Each time Christopher's head bounced off the ground, forming a dent and cracking the cement foundation, blood flying everywhere and coating Sam's hands, arms, and face with dark crimson liquid.

"I should have killed you years ago. You were always a pain in my ass!" Sam said, screaming as he was punching and slamming Christopher's head to the ground as Christopher's brains slid halfway out of his skull.

"Dad!" Jenny screamed and ran toward him. Kaliea was there and grabbed her by the hair. She flung her toward the other two slimy creatures, so that she landed right at their feet. She could hear the whispers.

"*Kill her, kill her.*"

"*She is the niece of Cadence.*"

"*She smells delicious.*"

Kaliea clapped vigorously, short and fast, giggling like a little child.

Meadow threw white lightning at Kaliea as tendrils grabbed her by the arms. Graves grabbed her by the head. He punched her, breaking her nose and taking a few teeth, along with some satisfaction. He turned and ran toward Jenny, getting there before the creatures grabbed her.

Graves kicked the one closest to her, sending it flying into the brick wall as it flopped around like a big jelly blob. The top layer of bricks rocked back and forth, giving way and piling on top of the creature, smashing its skull open, spilling out all the black gooey blood. Brains oozed out from underneath the debris, then it all turned to black ash. The other slimy shape swiped at Graves's head. He ducked and spun to his right, falling in behind the creature. He set his pistol to the back of its head and pulled the trigger. The bullet spun through the barrel, entering the back side of its head, blowing out the front of its skull, leaving only its bottom jaw. The tongue wiggled back and forth with black blood spilling out all over the lower half of the creature, and then — black ash.

Meanwhile, behind Graves, Meadow picked Kaliea up with her lightning tendrils and bounced her off the brick walls. She screamed at the impact.

Isabella ran to one side of the church to protect the dagger. Meadow broke the shackles binding her wrists, where she had stood motionless since the beginning. Meadow ran toward her father with a wild look in her eyes. Then, right before she got there, bolts of orange-red fire lightning hit Sam, grabbing him by the head, and wrapped around his body, lifting him up. Sam screamed, feeling the lightning getting tighter. Meadow followed the lightning trail. She found the other end attached to Cadence as he stood with hatred in his eyes, hatred unlike she had ever seen before.

***

Cadence was dreaming, lying in bed. Meadow stroked his chest. "You are special, Cady. I can feel it in you."

Isabella tucked her little Cadence into bed, put her hand on his cheek. "One day, my sweet little Cade, you will be exceptional; you are special." She reached down and kissed his forehead.

Christopher begged with hope. "Cadence, please help me. I need to kill myself. Trust me. I have a good plan. I figured out how to bring our mother back to us. You are the special one, not me. Things will happen to you once I am dead. You will not understand at first. Just accept it as it comes. My daughter, in time, please explain to her why I did this, and that I love her. If I don't survive this, I trust you to help her grow up and be strong and teach her our ways. Remember, I love you, and I hope to see you again. You are special; trust yourself and no one else."

***

Cadence stood there, head down, arms by his side, his forearms out in front and his hands gripped into fists. His face was covered in shadows, a slight trembling building up from the ground. His lightning was still squeezing Sam's body even tighter as he floated there, suspended in the air.

"Cade — what's happening?" Meadow's voice was soft and sweet as she touched his arm. Her fingertips burned to the touch of his skin. She pulled away quickly. "Cady!"

His arms folded at the elbows. He opened his fists as he pulled even tighter on the fire lightning ropes. Sam's screams began to muffle as breath escaped his lungs. Cadence gnashed his teeth as his lips curled back; his eyes turned a fiery orange-red. Sam could only look at Cadence while remaining helpless, floating in the air. Kaliea cowered in the corner behind the shadows.

Cadence shook, the fire growing intense around the lightning surrounding his body. He slammed his arms out wide to his side, gripping the lightning ropes. Jenny and Graves shielded their faces from the intense heat and glow emanating from Cadence's body. Sam's eyes widened as he screamed out.

"I always knew you were the strong one, Cadence — more powerful than my daughters, and that weak, annoying brother of yours. They were all so frightened, but not you — not you," Sam said, while looking at Cadence. He smiled, blood-covered teeth dripping from his mouth.

"Even stronger than you, Sam." Cadence quickly pulled back his arms and fell to one knee in a single, jerking motion. Sam's body ripped in half, flying in different directions. Blood, intestines, and all inner body parts spread out everywhere, covering the area.

"Father, no!" Kaliea screamed. She flew across the church and grabbed Cadence from behind. Then she pulled her arm back and slammed it through his back and out through his chest. She stood there holding his heart, still beating in her hand.

"I hate you! You motherfucker!" she screamed in his ear. "Try to come back now without your heart, you piece of shit." She pulled her arm back through his body. Still holding the heart, then opened her mouth and took a bite from the fleshy muscle, then a second bite, and a third. She chewed it and swallowed the chunks of flesh with a delicious smile on her bloody lips, blood trailing from her chin down her neck. She threw the remains of the heart to the ground and stomped on it, squashing it beneath her feet.

Jenny and Isabella both screamed simultaneously. Isabella ran over to Cadence as he fell to his knees; Jenny ran to her father.

The last two slimy creatures were standing behind Kaliea. The first one grabbed her.

"What are you doing?" Kaliea stood there, surprised. The second creature opened its mouth as it stretched out the size of her body. It engulfed her from the top of her head halfway down and bit her in half. Swallowing her from head to waist, the bottom half of her spewed black, crimson blood everywhere. A pool of mess, innards, intestines, and flesh flopped all over as wet slapping sounds hit the ground. The two remaining slimy creatures stood there.

"Cadence is dead. We need to eat; off to eat more."
The slimy creatures turned and disappeared.

***

Graves looked around the broken church, then at Meadow, and said with his arms out, "What the hell?"

Epilogue
Feeling the Power

Graves looked around in disbelief, thinking to himself, *Nobody will ever believe this, not even the guys back in Montana.*

Meadow knelt over Cadence with Isabella by her side; both were crying. Isabella thought for a moment, then reached under her cloak and pulled out the velvet bag with the dagger inside.

"This is the only way, child — trust me."

She removed the dagger from the velvet bag, put the tip of the blade in place, and slid it into Cadence's chest. The dagger drained his blood toward one of the two remaining empty skulls.

"I love you, my son." Isabella kissed his forehead. She stood and somberly made her way over to Christopher. Meadow kept crying uncontrollably, looking down at Cadence.

"Cady, I thought — hell, we all thought — you couldn't die. I keep waiting for you to wake up. Please, wake up." She pulled her hand off his chest and leaned back. Meadow stared down at her hands and licked the blood dripping from her palms as it swirled around her tongue, her face surrounded by a light-blue misty glow.

Blue veins appeared on her face and traveled down her neck. A few seconds later, they all disappeared.

"Daddy?" Jenny cried, holding her father's hand. "Please don't leave me again."

Isabella put her arms around Jenny and pulled her close. "My beautiful grand-daughter, it will be all right." She showed Jenny the dagger. "We can bring him back in time, and your Uncle Cade."

Jenny stared down at the dagger she was holding in her hand. "That will bring them back?"

"Yes, honey," Isabella smiled.

Jenny smiled back and sniffed up the snot ropes trailing down over her upper lip. Isabella made a slight crinkle of her nose and turned away.

"Here, let me." She moved in closer to her son and gasped at seeing him. He was unrecognizable, his face so beaten and bloody, with flesh hanging off the facial bone. His nose was flat to one side; his right eyeball hung down by the vein that connected to the brain, and the top of his head had brains exposed and sitting on the concrete floor. She wiped her tears from her face, took the dagger, and slid it into Christopher's chest as far as the blade could go. The blood swirled around the blade as it moved up to the third and final skull. Christopher moved and jerked as his soul separated and mixed with the blood sucked up into the dagger.

***

"So, your name is Graves," Meadow said, nodding her head. "You did good tonight. Now I know why Cadence brought you along. He was always a great judge of character."

"Thank you," Graves said, still looking around the broken church. "Now — can you please tell me what the hell happened here tonight? Where the hell did those little fat, funny, walking, slimy creatures go?"

With a little snort, Meadow said, "In time you will understand, and you will become a mentor and train the new protector. Cadence told me he saw this in you."

"Saw what in me — and what's a protector?" Graves said.

"You'll understand in time. Now, go to your girlfriend; she needs your comfort."

Isabella pushed back from hugging Jenny and her hands gripped Jenny's shoulders. She was looking at her beautiful grand-daughter.

"I cannot stay. I need to set the balance back between the darkness and us, and this dagger bares their souls. I will keep it safe. When it's time, I will resurrect them both."

Jenny cried and hugged her grandmother again. "Please help them. I need my father and uncle back. I don't know what to do without them."

"I promise, and I will check in on you from time to time." Isabella backed up into the shadows of the broken church. "I love you, my beautiful grand-daughter. And you, Mr Graves Hassin — please watch over her." She melted into the shadows until she disappeared.

Suddenly, Cadence's body jerked. Simultaneously, Christopher's body jerked. Christopher's body shot forth cold hard ice that swirled around in the empty air; the swirl pulled back and shot straight into Jenny's body. She fell to her knees. She jolted back in a quick motion as the ice turned her veins blue, and then quickly she snapped forward, her hair down in front of her face, her skin a blue texture. From Cadence's body came a ferocious fire, swirling around the empty air as it shot into Jenny's body. Without her taking a breath, she jolted back again as the fire turned her veins an orange-red. She snapped forward. She was panting and out of breath, and a fire surrounded her blue skin.

"Oh, God!" Graves ran to her side and grabbed her. "What's happening?" He turned to Meadow, looking for answers. Jenny saw Meadow standing lurking in the shadows.

"Why are you here?" Jenny's voice was a slow whisper, still panting.

"I am not my sisters. I love your uncle!" Meadow barked out a plea. "Please let me help you. In time, I can help you learn and understand what has happened here tonight. Your father and uncle chose you. Dark forces are coming. You will need to be ready."

Jenny, on her knees, grabbed her head with both hands, screaming. "It hurts!" Her arms pulled back behind her, both outstretched, fists formed tightly. She looked up, "Argh!" Her eyes suddenly opened. Her right eye was ice-cold with white-blue lightning licking around it. Her left eye was an orange-red fire with lightning licking around it. She screamed again, staring up at the new dawn peeking through, seeing all the shadows and demons flying around and above her — different shapes of souls, some scary, some pleasant, but they all scared her. Her eyes glowed as her right hand began to form ice lightning, and her left hand, sparked fire lightning.

Graves and Meadow stood there, staring at her. They turned and looked at each other.

The End

Coming Soon

Book Two
The Three-Headed Dagger
and the King's Son

www.ingramcontent.com/pod-product-compliance
Lightning Source LLC
Chambersburg PA
CBHW021328190726
48288CB00003B/1007